The Child's Concept of Story

Arthur N. Applebee

The Child's Concept of Story

Ages Two to Seventeen

The University of
Chicago Press
Chicago and London

Arthur N. Applebee, who holds degrees from
Yale University, Harvard University, and the
University of London, is the author of *Tradition
and Reform in the Teaching of English* and
numerous articles in professional journals.

The University of Chicago Press, Chicago 60637
The University of Chicago Press, Ltd., London

©1978 by The University of Chicago
All rights reserved. Published 1978
Printed in the United States of America
83 82 81 80   9 8 7 6 5 4 3 2

Library of Congress Cataloging in Publication Data

Applebee, Arthur N
   The child's concept of story.

   Bibliography: p.
   Includes index.
   1. Children's stories—Psychological aspects.
2. Cognition in children.   3. Children—Language.
I. Title.
BF723.S74A66   801'.3   77-8309

ISBN 0–226–02117–3 (cloth)
ISBN 0–226–02118–1 (paper)

Contents

List of Figures and Tables

Acknowledgments

The studies which follow began as part of a doctoral thesis at the University of London; these have been modified and I hope enriched by several years of reflection and reformulation of the results. There are always many debts in such an undertaking; if they cannot be repaid they can at least be acknowledged.

The primary debt is to James N. Britton, who has been both advisor and friend at all stages in this work. His influence on all that follows is greater than footnotes and acknowledgments can ever make clear, but it will be evident to all who know him and his work.

The second debt is to the students and staff of the six schools in which data were gathered during the various main and preliminary studies. All made me welcome and unhesitatingly provided the facilities and time needed for the investigation.

The third debt is to my wife, Marcia Lynn Applebee, who has cheerfully shared her own knowledge of primary school children, and opened the doors of her classrooms to my not always helpful presence. In the process of reading the various drafts of the manuscript itself, she has wielded a wicked blue pencil.

The final debt is to all of our family and friends, who continue to speak to us in spite of the preoccupation that work on this book has sometimes involved.

One

Introduction

The Organization of the Book

This book is concerned with the area of language use which is usually called "literature," and, more particularly, with the interaction of children and stories. To place this interaction within a broader perspective, we will begin, in this and the following chapter, by exploring the uses of language, and some of the relationships of these uses to general processes of mind. These chapters may be of most interest to theoretically oriented readers. Later chapters focus more specifically on children and stories, turning to a series of empirical studies of storytelling and response to literature to amplify and clarify the theoretical perspective adopted. The presentation tries to strike a balance that will be acceptable both to the teacher and to the research worker. The emphasis in the text is on a coherent presentation of what has been learned about children's expectations about stories; footnotes and appendixes are used to provide more detailed information about the collection and analysis of data.

Chapters 3, 4, and 5 explore the child's concept of what stories are, how they can be organized, and why they are told, as revealed primarily in the stories children tell; they will be the chapters of most interest to readers concerned with primary school children. Chapters 6 and 7 shift the emphasis toward children's responses to particular stories, and the way in which those responses are related to general stages of mental development. These chapters, particularly chapter 7, will be the ones of most interest to readers concerned with adolescents and college students. The final chapter returns to the more general framework developed at the beginning of the book.

Representation of Experience

What we will be seeking in the first two chapters is a model of various ways of using language. The search for such a model is itself a characteristic, albeit somewhat self-conscious, example of the usual relationship between individuals and their experience.

Whatever our age, whatever our language, whatever our cultural background, we function psychologically by building systematic *representations* of experience, which provide both an interpretation (or structuring) of the past and a system for anticipating the future. This is hardly a new observation, but it is central to an understanding of language and its various uses.

How to describe these "representations of experience" is the primary issue which divides competing schools of psychology. For our purposes, it is enough to recognize that a system of representation is a mental record of our past experience. (More technically, it is *a system of implications of previous activity,* where the "implications" are a structural pattern imposed on the matrix of mind in the course of the activity itself.) This record will include the context of the activity: the events which precede and follow it, as well as those which occur at the same time. Each new experience will modify the record, or representation, which we have been constructing. For those aspects of the experience which repeat themselves the implications will grow stronger; those that change or are contradicted will weaken the corresponding implications. Our representations provide more, however, than just a regularly updated archive of our past; they also provide a set of reasonable expectations to guide us in interpreting and reacting to new experience. That which has occurred before, we expect—in similar circumstances—to occur again; we rely on such constancy and consistency to gain mastery and control.

Piaget[1] has described two distinct though interrelated processes which are involved in any new experience. The first, which he calls "assimilation," is the process by which a new object or behavior is integrated into an existing record or representation; it is thus given meaning or purpose, is "defined as" something in our world. The second process, "accommodation," involves the changes which are necessary in our representation if the new experience is to be interpreted in that way. (Consider children of four or five hearing a fairy tale. They will *assimilate* the story to their past experience of similar tales, providing themselves with expectations about such things as types of characters, patterns of behavior, and suitable endings. On the other hand, their understanding of "fairy tales" will be somewhat altered and expanded by the new characters and actions which they meet in the particular tale; these changes are what Piaget means by *accommodation*.)

It is because we understand "reality" only in terms of our own, unique representations that it is possible to talk of the child's "construction of reality" (Berger and Luckmann 1966). In a very real sense, we *build* the world through our accumulated record of experience, our systems of implications of previous activity. The adequacy of these representations is a crucial factor in determining our ability to function in that world: an adequate representation will allow us to understand and to some extent control what happens to us; an inadequate one will leave us subject to William James' "booming, buzzing confusion."

We need to remind ourselves, however, that the representations we have been describing operate, in Polanyi's (1958) terms, *tacitly*: our attention is focused *through* them *to* a goal. Because we do not focus on them directly, we are often completely unaware of their nature, and may be unable to describe them accurately even if we wish to do so. George Kelly's (1955) discussion of personal construct theory has played an important role in shaping the theory which underlies the studies in this book, so it is worth considering Kelly's notions briefly here. Kelly analyzes our representations of the world as consisting of sets of bipolar *constructs* with definite patterns of implications between them. Taking the activity of the scientist as a suitable model of psychological processes in general,[2] Kelly argues that when we are using our construct system we are constantly "testing hypotheses" about the nature of the world. The point is that a construct "channelizes" or governs a person's behavior, and that channeled in this way, every action becomes a test of the validity of the construct itself. In our terms this is simply to say that every action is guided by the implications of previous activity and will have implications of its own: the former provide the "hypothesis" and the latter the "test." Thus "hypothesis testing" is really metaphoric; the processes we are describing need involve no conscious processes or explicit awareness of alternatives. What they do involve is a meaning-assigning act of integration, an ordering of the elements of the world in a pattern with implications that will give us a measure of understanding and control.

We spend our lives adding to and refining our systems of representation, perfecting our models of reality as our store of knowledge and experience increases. These models take many forms, which in adulthood supplement and enrich one another though for the child they only gradually become accessible. The earliest form of representation is "enactive"; it takes its structure from direct action and begins with the infant's first attempts at coordinated movement and response. The second form of representation is "iconic"; it is closest to a model in the usual sense, providing an image or pattern which reflects the distinctive features of the represented experience. The third form of representation is "symbolic," and it is from this that all of the highly elaborated and powerful systems of knowledge which we have evolved derive.[3] It is with this third form that we will be most interested in our consideration of language, but here too we will find a gradual development, marked by characteristic stages in the organization of the symbolic representation itself.

The Social Context

Though each of us constructs our own representation of the world out of our encounters with it, these encounters are embedded within a social milieu which has a consistent structure of its own. For the infant, the first and most important social relationship is with an adult who will respond patiently and consistently to the child's actions; it is this encounter which leads the infant eventually to expect "reciprocity," to have an assurance that his or her actions will provoke a response. Reciprocity is central in the development of symbolic systems, for it produces gestures which are intended to evoke a response from another person. These gestures are gradually conventionalized and simplified, becoming more and more controlled and intentional, so that long before language as such emerges, a highly elaborate and effective system of communication will be evident between the child and the responsive adult (Bruner 1968). When, much later, the child speaks its first words, they will be simply an extension of processes already comfortably under way (Bruner 1975).

The social context in which the individual learns the rules of language insures that the "proper" rules are learned, those which will allow effective functioning in the social context itself. What each of us must do is build our own representation—our own model—of the rules of language, extending and correcting it as we gain experience in its use. This language is eventually superimposed on the nonverbal communication out of which it grows, enriching and extending the communication itself; but the characteristic elements of reciprocity and mutual understanding always play a central role.

The Expressive Mode

These first forms of language, used under conditions of reciprocity, are the beginning of what James Britton (1970) has called the "expressive mode" of language use. The central feature of this mode is that the participants are able to rely on a shared representation of experience, usually one that has been built up out of a context of shared interests, mutual experience, and common goals and objectives. Since the representation is shared, there need be little explicit consideration of it. Instead the language seems concerned primarily with the *self,* expressing the attitudes and feelings of the speaker or writer. Much of this expressiveness derives originally from nonlinguistic features—from the eye contact, facial expressions, posture, and gestures that are an important part of the reciprocity of the face-to-face encounter for the adult as well as for the child.[4] Much, too, derives from intonation patterns and inflections which have little to do with the overt "subject matter" (or referential meaning) of the talk. Still the seeming focus on the self can be misleading: the concern in expressive talk is often with assimilating experience into the shared framework, a process in which the expression of attitudes and feelings is a kind of shorthand for monitoring the progress and direction of assimilation, rather than an end in itself.

Britton (1969) has presented lengthy transcripts of conversation in the expressive mode, summing up at the end of one of them:

The language remains "expressive" throughout, in the sense that it is relaxed, self-presenting, self-revealing, addressed to a few intimate companions; in the sense that it moves easily from general comment to narration of particular experiences and back again; and in the special sense that in making comments the speakers do not aim at accurate, explicit reference (as one might in an argument or sociological report) and in relating experience they do not aim at a polished performance (as a raconteur or a novelist would). (P. 96)

Britton's emphasis is on the self-revealing aspects of the talk he is analyzing, but this self-expression is clearly in the service of a larger goal: in this case the goal of coming to terms with a Hemingway short story. The girls in the transcripts reveal their thoughts and feelings to one another largely to have them sanctioned by the group, to be reassured, as one of them puts it, that "that's part of growing up" (p. 92), and at the same time to increase their own understanding of the story. The other aspects—the fluidity, informal style, and lack of conscious direction—are all related to the extent to which the expressive assumes a common representation or world view from the start. The girls understand one another quite well, reacting in very much the same way to one another's comments; and it is this common culture, this representation of experience, that they are "working on" in their expressive talk, maintaining and at the same time extending and refining it in light of the story. In the end, they will have fitted the story into their world view, assimilated it, and come to an understanding of its message. In a very real sense, they will have *given it* the meaning which it will have for them.

When we seek to move beyond the commonsense, taken for granted world of the expressive, the language used will be subject to new demands if we are to continue to understand one another. This leads in turn to other, more specialized forms of language, which we will be considering in the next chapter.

Two

The Uses of Language

Introduction

The expressive is a central mode of language use, both developmentally and generically. Nonetheless, the assumption of a shared representation of experience which gives the expressive its power also limits its usefulness; as soon as the assumption of a shared world becomes less tenable, other modes of language use become necessary. These differentiated uses of language will be our concern in this chapter.[1]

The first major dimension of differentiation in the use of language represents a continuum of techniques of symbolization which culminate at the extremes in, roughly, "pure logic" and "pure poetry." This distinction has often been made on the basis of the formal properties of the language involved (for example, Langer 1942; Burke 1966; Sapir 1966), but we will be arguing that these formal properties are linked to underlying psychological processes.

Subjective and Objective

As a prelude to our study of "pure logic" and "pure poetry," however, it will help to consider briefly Susanne Langer's (1967, 1972) monumental study, *Mind*. In this work, she argues that there is a fundamental unity in all felt experience: such diverse phenomena as cognition, perception, and emotion differ primarily in their origins, not in the basic psychological processes involved. We have, on the one hand, feelings which arise out of contact between the individual and his or her surrounding environment, and on the other, feelings which arise as the result of internal processes. Langer calls feeling which arises as the direct result of the impact of outside events, *objective,* and that which arises out of internal activity, *subjective.*

Though both subjective and objective feeling are based on similar psychological processes, we tend to treat our experience of them as belonging to two distinct realms. They are the worlds of the self and not-self, personal and public, emotional and rational.

Since we construct our representations of the world out of the implications of our past experience, it is not surprising to find that quite different techniques of representation have evolved in the two domains. As we shall see in a moment, those techniques which have evolved in the objective domain culminate in what we have been calling "pure logic," while those in the subjective domain culminate in what we have been calling "pure poetry." Both lead to highly developed symbolic systems which allow us to build and share representations of one or another aspect of our experience, opening for discussion and public consideration what would otherwise remain very private constructs. Language is central in both cases, but it is language which is subject to very different constraints and conventions.

Language and Objective Experience

The characteristic of objective experience is that it seems to originate outside of the individual, and from there to impinge on each of us in similar ways. With language we achieve such objectivity by stating the rules of argument and language use as fully as possible, either in the course of the argument itself or by reliance on a *context* of "relevant conventions, beliefs, and presuppositions 'taken for granted' by members of the speech community" (Lyons 1969, p. 413). Abstract logical and mathematical systems represent perhaps the fullest development of this type of symbolization; the necessary premises and rules of use are explicitly laid out, and differ from one logical or mathematical system to another. The careful specification of the rules and premises makes them "objective" and "external" in a way that such rules for symbolization usually are not. Though individuals will differ in their mastery of the system, they will all be using the same rules and conventions, and should reach much the same conclusions: any argument or representation which is produced will be subject to verification against the formalized rules.

Although Polanyi (1958) has demonstrated that there is always a tacit, personal component in even the most rigorous formal system, this component can be reduced to the point that the system *seems* to convey a totally objective "meaning." Following Britton (1970), we will call language which reduces the personal component in this way *transactional,* since this kind of objectivity is the condition for transactions between people who do not share a world in common, for the development of theory as well as for the day-to-day business of life.

Implicit Formalization

Symbolic logic and abstract mathematical systems represent one pole of transactional symbolism, but there are also many intermediate modes which draw on a less explicit formalization provided by the general context in which the discussion is occurring. This is a large class of the transactional, including most historical, philosophical, and scientific writing—Darwin's *The Origin of Species* as well as Langer's *Mind* and Durant's *Story of Civilization.* Such works are validated against a background of rules of evidence and accepted procedures which govern their own specialized disciplines, rather than against the formal axioms and operations of symbolic logic.[2] Kuhn (1962) has given detailed attention to the special conventions of professional life within the various fields of science, discussing them as "paradigms" governing inquiry. Such paradigms, which change over time and which are rarely fully formulated, con-stitute a formalization of a higher order than would be ap-parent from examining a single discourse in isolation from the professional context from which it derives.

The individual's knowledge of such paradigms develops out of his or her experience within the professional context. To the extent that there is a paradigm structuring the behavior of people in a given profession, their behavior will have a structure and consistency reflecting that paradigm. In turn, this structure will insure that actions have a consistent system of implications (in the sense of the previous chapter), a system that *is* knowledge of the paradigms involved. The acquisition of syntax is a good example of the process in a nonprofessional context: after centuries of study, scholars still disagree on the nature and structure of language—though they make skilled use of its rules even as they attempt to describe them. The learning of such systems of implicit rules is part of what scholars call the "primary socialization" of childhood, as well as part of the "secondary socialization" which takes place as we enter the more specialized contexts of scientific and professional endeavor (Berger and Luckmann 1966). In turn, these rules give us our first socially derived experiences of objectivity, of a world that seems external and absolute even though many of its forms are socially derived and arbitrary.

Language and Subjective Experience

Transactional techniques are relatively well understood, in part because one of their most characteristic forms involves the explicit statement of rules of use. Because they are specified in the course of the argument, however, these rules need have little to do with a person's normal approaches to experience; they can remain unrelated to processes governing more general patterns of construing because they are quite literally built up outside of the person using them.[3] The subjective, on the other hand, is a product of the internal working of the mind, and must reflect the normal and complex processes of that mind more directly. The constructs involved will be neither specified nor ordinarily fully specifiable—they are systems of implications built up independently by each individual. Rather than an external, objective, impersonal conclusion, a work which attempts to symbolize subjective experience leads to a complex, slow, internal formulation of the relationships among constructs.

Again following Britton (1970), we will call language which leads to such personal, subjective patterns of response *poetic,* since it is in the language of poetry that the possibilities of this mode of symbolization are usually most fully realized.[4]

Though the poetic techniques through which such complex experience is symbolized are less clearly understood than those of transactional writing, it is clear that such symbolization relies on the establishment of significant relationships among the various parts of a work. Kenneth Burke's (1966) discussions of literature are helpful in understanding the processes involved. He argues that the structure and form of a work are shaped by a system of "personal equations" or attitudes toward life. These personal equations originate with the author; they reflect his or her own representation of experience, and in turn give structure to the experiences depicted in the work. The reader is then able to "read back" these equations from the systems of relationships within the work itself. In essence, the work provides an artifactual record of a particular representation of experience, much as the growth rings in a tree trunk provide an artifactual record of seasons past. The constructs shaping the work will function at many levels, ranging all the way from those which govern the consistency of each individual character in a story to such general principles as Fate or Justice or Destiny (themselves reflected in complex interrelationships among the characters and incidents).

To "read back" the personal equations that structure a work is to build a representation of the construct system which shaped it. There are no formalized, objective rules to apply, and no taken for granted context to specify the proper reactions. Indeed, if we examine the reactions of individual readers closely, we will find that each creates his or her own unique reconstruction out of the material which the text provides (Holland 1975). The closest that we can come to objective rules of interpretation are the principles formulated by the literary critic, but as Frye (1957) has warned, criticism can account for a literary experience or value judgment but always remains something other than the literary experience itself: "However disciplined by taste and skill, the experience of literature is, like literature itself, unable to speak" (p. 27).

Although this experience is internal and personal, there is a sense in which it remains controlled by the structure of the work. Holland (1975) has noted the possibility of total self-delusion, but in general if a reader's reaction wanders too far from the author's, the rest of the patterns of interrelationships within the work will begin to break down. This in turn will force the reader to reformulate his or her reaction, searching for a pattern that will lead to fewer inconsistencies in the texture of the work. It is because of this restriction achieved through the shaping of the presented experience that poetic symbolization can still lead to interpersonal consistency in response.

The central role of structure in poetic symbolization means that the rules of use are concerned in large measure with specifying the relationships which count as significant. Unlike the essentially linear, analytic structure of transactional language, however, these relationships occur at many different levels simultaneously. The phonemic, semantic, syntactic, and thematic structures of a poem, for example, will be inextricably interwoven to produce an "import" which can never be transactionally paraphrased.

The purest instances of poetic techniques are, as the name suggests, largely works of poetry. It is in this genre that the system of constructs with which the author is working is most fully projected in the form, and hence in this genre that there is the fullest control of the subjective construal of experience. There are also many works in other genres which achieve a similar control, but in which the primary source of this control shifts from words and sounds to larger units—scenes, characters, incidents—which may themselves be built up out of word-by-word detail.[5] Such works are also poetic in our sense, providing an effective symbolization of subjective feeling through a careful structuring of the presented experience.

There are, of course, many intermediate forms of the poetic, just as there are of the transactional. In many works, poetic techniques are used to control only those aspects of the reader's response which are essential to a particular "theme" or purpose. Such works are often one-dimensional, but this one dimension may be well and clearly drawn; we do not necessarily reject a book out of hand because it is not "complex" enough. As examples we can cite much popular fiction, the James Bond novels, science fiction and mystery stories, and most didactic literature—Orwell's *Animal Farm* as well as Bunyan's *Pilgrim's Progress*. The constructs which are projected in the form tend to be restricted to those necessary, for example, to the suspense in a mystery, the conflict in an adventure, the triumph of love in a romance. The rest of the reader's response is assumed to correspond to conventional modes of construing, with little attempt at elaboration or further poetic control.

Participant and Spectator

A mixture of poetic and transactional technique is, in fact, quite characteristic of most uses of language; it is rare to find either in a pure form. Yet though they are often mixed, the conventions of the two types of symbolization are to some extent in conflict. This is because poetic techniques ask us to consider a work as a whole; as Smith (1968) has argued, it is only at the end that the total pattern is revealed. Our attitude toward such an experience becomes that of a *spectator:* we look on, testing our hypotheses about structure and meaning, but we do not rush in to interrupt—to do so would obscure the relationships and spoil the effect of the whole.[6]

The techniques of transactional symbolism, on the other hand, lead us to *participate* more directly in the experience being offered: we judge it step by step, and act on it piecemeal— whether that action is taking place in the realm of everyday life (close the door, please) or in the more intellectual realms of theoretical argument or professional discussion.

The "wholeness" of discourse in the spectator role, and its contrast with participant-role language, is perhaps most evident in the ways we respond to it. With transactional discourse, we usually respond by continuing the discussion already under way—we qualify, accept, or challenge the argument, offer a new perspective, or simply express our pleasure or disgust. We respond, in other words, with more transactional language. With poetic discourse, however, a poetic response is relatively rare, and when it does occur it does not form a continuing dialogue in the way that a series of transactional arguments or statements may. At most, it will be another contribution to the same literary tradition. Usually when we start to formulate our response to a work in the spectator role, we move out of it into transactional, participant-role writing or speech. We try to find an objective symbolization for the subjective experience we have had, in order both to share and to clarify our responses.

This is an important point, and an easy place for confusion: when we talk about poetic language, the language we use is usually transactional. If we look, as we will in later chapters, at the development of literary response by considering what children say about stories, we do it by looking "through" their transactional language to the subjective response the child is trying to describe. We do not, in such cases, sample spectator-role language directly.

D. W. Harding (1937) has commented perceptively on the profound difference in outlook which results from our choice of spectator or participant roles. He argues that when one is just "looking on," one is able to evaluate an event in a way that a participant cannot; if the onlooker is more detached, less involved, he or she is also more comprehensive in point of view. Experiences in the spectator role thus become experiences in which our various systems of representation can become fully involved and integrated, because there is no need to mobilize any one of them for immediate action. The participant, on the other hand, is called on to use values, beliefs, and modes of action toward more immediate ends. Rather than a full response, the participant must usually offer a more rapid, focused one which will allow events to be "handled" or "survived" or "controlled." As we move further from the direct experience with which Harding begins, the participant-role activities of professional discourse and theory building become more meditative and complex, but they continue to use language as a tool applied to a problem in need of solution. This language remains focused and limited, relying on processes of definition and delimitation, analysis and argument, which are the basis of transactional symbolization. Such uses of language in effect prohibit the full but multidimensional response which the spectator role invites.[7]

These differences mean that we cannot simultaneously adopt the roles of both the spectator and the participant. Even a work which mixes transactional and poetic techniques (as most do) has to be experienced either as a whole, or step by step. Still the choice of role is not arbitrary; like other aspects of language use, it is governed by conventions which indicate the appropriate manner of approach to the work as a whole. Such conventions usually operate below the level of consciousness; we adjust our expectations automatically as we move, for example, from a short story to an article in a professional journal. The strength of these expectations is perhaps most apparent on those occasions when we deliberately ignore them. Thus we may read Defoe's *Journal of the Plague Year* as a work of literature, or we may decide to treat it as a source of information about the plague. In the first case we are using it in the spectator role; in the second, in the participant. The shift this brings about is dramatic: in the spectator role we may find it an exciting tale, but in the participant role throw it away in disgust when we discover that it is not the firsthand account that it purports to be. We ask different questions of works in the two roles, bring different criteria to bear on them, and take away quite different impressions.[8] Though both roles are important in individual and cultural development, it is the spectator role, in all of its various forms, which is the primary concern of the present study.

The Continuum

The distinction between participant and spectator roles operates at the level of a work as a whole, in effect functioning as a super-ordinate system of rules structuring our reaction to the more specific detail. In terms of transactional and poetic symbolization, almost all works will show a mix: it is usually a question of degree of subjectivity or objectivity, rather than of a choice between them. This mixture helps to insure that our subjective and objective representations of experience remain in alignment, an alignment which in turn can be used by an author. In the participant role, "persuasive" or "rhetorical" techniques represent an appeal to subjective feeling to bolster what (by virtue of its participant-role status) claims to be objective argument. Far from weakening an argument, such appeals usually strengthen it, demonstrating a congruence between the objective and subjective experiences with which it is dealing. This congruence or "sense of fitness" may carry the reader over weak points as well as counter prior allegiances to conflicting points of view.[9] Still, the rhetoric will work only if it is a successful integration of the two realms of experience. "Only those voices from without are effective," as Kenneth Burke (1950) put it, "which speak in the language of a voice within" (p. 39).

This puts concern with "abuses" of language through propaganda and rhetoric in a somewhat different light. If in fact such works are effective because they mesh with our personal constructs, then the danger lies not in the communication but in the constructs themselves. We may be justified in complaining that someone is appealing to our baser instincts, but the unpalatable fact is that they are *our* instincts, and not ones that have been created for us. Education in such circumstances might better focus on the developing personality and values of the students, than on "proper uses of language."

In the spectator role, transactional devices will be used to retain control of aspects of response not firmly controlled by the poetic form—to set a scene, describe a character, and sometimes to draw a moral or summarize the "point." Such techniques orient the reader, but they are successful only when they are consistent with the subjective, personal response simultaneously being shaped by the work as a whole. The test of the transactional symbol will no longer be its truth or accuracy against the background of an objective system, but its consistency and placement within the poetic system of interrelationships among the various parts of the work.

The Elaborative Choice

The poetic-transactional continuum with its underlying contrast between subjective and objective realms of experience helps us understand the differing techniques of symbolization, but it does not carry us far in analyzing the effects of these experiences on our manner of construing. Kelly (1955) has argued that such effects normally take the form of a cycle in which an extension or reformulation of the system of representation to include new elements is followed by a period of redefinition and mastery within the constraints of that extension. The tacit decision whether to extend the system or to work out the implications within the present limits is what he has called the elaborative choice. This choice is ordinarily governed by whether further mastery of old elements or the addition of new factors is more likely to lead to increased control. Both processes are valuable: if a system simply extended its range without working through the implications, it would quickly become unworkable; if it never extended its range it would be unable to adjust to changing circumstances or to extend its control to new areas.

Bruner's (1968, 1973) studies of infants provide many simple,

concrete examples of such a "choice" in operation at an unconscious level. In one series of investigations, children of ten
to twelve weeks were found to "swipe" at an object held within
reach, with fist tightly closed and elbow locked. By three-
and-a-half to four months, babies would reach with hands
wide open, the reach closing when the object was at the midline of
the body, and the hands closing at contact. Even as late as seven
months, vision would be restricted to the period of launching the
reach, with gaze aversion or eye closing throughout the rest of the
action. Rigid joints, orientation around the midline of the body,
eye closing, and gaze aversion all serve to reduce the complexity
of the action to a manageable level. As the child becomes more
skillful within this limited context, the process is complicated by
making use of more resources: unclenching fists, bending elbows,
and finally keeping eyes open throughout the reach. Such processes of expansion and articulation parallel Kelly's notion of
the elaborative choice. They produce the well-known plateaus in
learning curves and represent very basic psychological processes.

Though our discussion will be complicated by the number of
differing systems of representation involved—those of the author,
those of the audience, and those projected in the work through
poetic or transactional techniques—we can distinguish a similar
contrast in various uses of language. It is a contrast between
situations where, as Holland (1968) puts it, "a writing closely
conforms to cultural values; where it directly challenges them"
(p. 335).

Reformulation

Those works which challenge a system of values, seeking to
extend its range or alter its basic principles, are concerned with
that aspect of the elaborative choice which we will call *reformulation*. *King Lear* and *The Origin of Species* are alike in
this respect: each posed a basic challenge to the system of beliefs
which formed the background against which it was written.
Spectator-role writings raise this challenge by seeking to create a
conflict within the subjective construal of the experience they
present; participant-role writings achieve a similar tension

through objective argument and explicit demonstration of contradiction or inadequacy.

For such works to lead to a reformulation of basic principles,
the audience must recognize and accept the relevance of the
experience to their own lives. Kelly's (1955) discussions of
psychotherapy provide us with a good model of the process; in the
following passage we can almost substitute "reader" for "client,"
"author" for "clinician," and "work" for "fixed role."

> As soon as the client begins to take the fixed role "seriously"
> he is likely to have difficulties and his progress is likely to slow
> down. In the successful case, it is when the client begins to say
> in some way, "I feel this is the way I really *am,* rather than,
> "I feel this is the way I *ought* to become," that the clinician
> notes other evidence of real progress. Sometimes this kind of
> "emotional insight" is voiced as, "I feel as if this had been the
> *real me* all the time but that I had never let myself realize it
> before." (P. 379)

In a similar way an author must make the audience respond,
"That's me" and "That's the way things are." The task is not an
easy one. Each reader will recreate the work in the process of
reading it, and will transform the meaning and significance to
suit his or her own unconscious purposes (Holland 1968, 1975).
If these purposes are badly thwarted, the work may simply be
rejected in disgust.

Kuhn (1962) deals with changes of the sort we are calling
reformulations as "scientific revolutions," fundamental shifts in
the paradigm governing the course of normal scientific inquiry.
As with spectator-role writing, he has emphasized that such shifts
depend on the intuitive reaction of the scientific community, a
reaction conditioned by the long experience and tacit knowledge
of those who have been working in the field. Unless the discourse
can generate a sense of "rightness and proportion," a feeling of
correspondence between its claims and the tacit knowledge of
these workers, the arguments will be set aside as anomalies which
the present theory does not handle well but which are tolerated
because of what the theory *is* able to do (much as the babies in
Bruner's [1968] studies "tolerate" the loss of information that
results from closing their eyes in reaching for a ball dangled in
front of them).

Articulation

At the opposite pole of the elaborative choice, we have works whose major concern is with *articulation* of a given set of constructs, working out their detailed implications within the limits that have been set by the general paradigm. As Kenneth Burke (1966) has pointed out, any system has a series of implications entailed in it, implications which we have a corresponding tendency to want to discover. To fully order our world, we must have a conception of both the perfect saint and the perfect villain, as well as of the more mundane characters with whom we are likely to come in contact. It is with formulating these extremes, with working through our systems of constructs to their logical conclusions, that much writing in both the spectator and participant roles is concerned.

The concern with providing a more or less definitive, fully articulated summation of an established system is best illustrated by Kuhn's (1962) discussion of textbooks. These seek not to change but to preserve and legitimate a set of beliefs (or principles or theories) so that they can be passed on intact to a new generation. In science the process is particularly clear, involving a process of reinterpreting the past to serve the purposes of the present—and inevitably distorting the past in the process.

In the spectator role, this pole of the elaborative choice is similarly marked by genres whose concern is largely with summation and ordering rather than with reformulation. Bettelheim (1976) points us toward one major set of examples when he notes that throughout our history, a child's intellectual life, "apart from immediate experiences within the family, depended on mythical and religious stories and fairy tales.... Myths and closely related religious legends offered material from which children formed their concepts of the world's origin and purpose, and of the social ideals a child could pattern himself after" (p. 24). Such stories could perform this function because, as Levi-Strauss (1966) has argued, the refinements of myth and ritual "are explicable by a concern for what one might call 'micro-adjustment'—the concern to assign every single creature, object or feature to a place within a class" (p. 10). Levi-Strauss' documentation of these points with evidence from primitive cultures is extensive and provides much detailed support for our sense that myth and ritual serve as cultural reference points. In our own culture, these functions are served by other media— among them advertising, if we accept Leymore's (1975) provocative analysis.[10]

The Continuum

Articulation and reformulation are two poles of a continuum with its center in the expressive, where we find a body of works which seek to integrate new experience into a common world view or representation of experience. In the participant role, this is the mode of giving information, whether in newspaper reports or mail-order catalogs. It is also the mode of consultation, of a sharing of viewpoints and attitudes when there is little concern with carrying a particular point—the sort of pooling of experience in which the girls in Britton's (1969) transcripts were engaging (p. 7, above). In the spectator role, we find at the center of the continuum a body of literature whose point seems to be that others find the world as we do, sharing the same problems and triumphs, heartbreak and joy. Boswell's journals, travelogues in general, most autobiography, and much biography would fall here; all in the end not making a point but celebrating our natural interest in one another.

There are also many works which fall between the expressive and the work which seeks to articulate or reformulate a major aspect of our experience. In the transactional mode, these works correspond to a large area of discourse which Kuhn (1962) has labeled "normal science." Here one pushes a system to its limits, working out its implications, coordinating and systematizing its parts. As such it represents the bulk of scientific and professional writing, a point which Kuhn captures when he calls it "normal." The process of articulating a paradigm is a long and difficult one, usually involving many people and varying perspectives over an extended period of time. It provides the essential context for reformulation as well as for articulation, for as Kuhn notes, it is only when a paradigm has been fully articulated, pushed to its limits, that its weaknesses as well as its possibilities become apparent. And when the faults become overriding, the field is ripe for revolution, for reformulation of the governing paradigm and a starting over within the new context.

From this perspective the large body of best-selling literature does not deserve the opprobrium usually heaped upon it. If we take Richards' (1924) point that best-sellers in all the arts exemplify "the most general levels of attitude development" (p. 203), then such works help us gain control and precision in a way that is analogous both to normal science and to a child's play while learning a new skill. The pleasure which such works offer is a pleasure of mastery, and just as a child becomes bored when the skill is mastered, dropping some elements from his or her play and taking up others, so too we can expect the reader to become bored once the principles underlying the stories have been mastered.[11] The formula novel is dull only when we know its formula; but when we do, we move on to works that offer a new challenge and hence the possibility of a new mastery.

Indwelling

It should be clear by now that in arguing a dimension corresponding to Kelly's notion of elaborative choice, we are not suggesting that the spectator role can be divided into those works which provide us with insight into ourselves and those which do not. The point we wish to make is that there is a qualitative difference in the *kind* of insight which is provided, a difference which lies in the way in which a work is implicitly to be construed. On the one hand we have works which are concerned with a struggle between differing representations of experience, with forcing us to expand and reformulate our views in order to begin again from a new set of basic principles. On the other hand, we have works concerned with the reconciliation of conflict within an accepted system of values, with rearranging and articulating its parts, bringing them into alignment with one another and ultimately confirming the system in broad outline even as it is reorganized and changed in its detail. Whether we are concerned with moving toward a new paradigm or with gaining mastery of the one which we have tentatively assumed, the arts remain one of our most important instruments. They are our mode of "indwelling" (Polanyi 1958), of ordering our mind and experience into a coherent and useful whole, an ordering that can only be done tacitly but which structures the whole of our active life.

In selecting examples in our discussion of the elaborative choice, we have treated them against the background of the time and place of their origin. This was a useful simplification while presenting the concept, but is not a constraint on its application. We can equally apply the elaborative choice in considering the effect of a work on its author, on a particular reader, or on society at large. Whichever focus we choose, we are likely to find major shifts over time. *The Origin of Species,* for example, led to a reformulation of the paradigm underlying the work of scholars in many different fields, yet partly because it was so successful it is today at most a somewhat dated reference point, an articulation of an accepted point of view. Similar processes occur in the spectator role: we have all had the experience of a book which once excited us, opening our eyes to whole new vistas of human experience, and yet which in later years seemed trite or superficial. Such changes are a natural outcome of the growth which the elaborative choice helps to foster.

The Expressive Center

When we bring together our two dimensions, we get a model of the uses of language such as that in figure 1. The expressive mode, introduced in the previous chapter, lies at the center of the model where there is an almost equal mix of objective and subjective modes of experience, and the language moves easily back and forth between them. Gossip—in Harding's (1962) sense of casually talking things over—is one of the clearest examples of this aspect of the expressive. We can tell a bit of a story, make a comment, offer a suggestion, all within the context of both the reciprocity and the shared representation of experience which are characteristic of the expressive. As Harding (1962) puts it, "The gossip implicitly invites us to agree that what he reports is interesting enough to deserve reporting and that the attitude he adopts, openly or tacitly, is an acceptable evaluation of events"

Figure 1   The Uses of Language

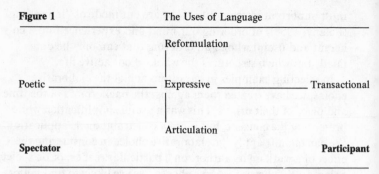

(p. 137). We can also move very easily out of the expressive, making the argument or information we are offering more explicit and precise, or becoming caught up in our story and developing its form and shape. In either case we have a speaker who assumes less about the listener's view of the world, a lessening of dependence on expressive cues, and a sharpening of poetic or transactional form.

The expressive also lacks the assimilative pressures of the two poles of the elaborative choice: it seeks to integrate new experience into a coherent representation of experience, but is fluid with respect to the form that integration should take. Either articulation or reformulation can easily result. Berger and Luckmann (1966) have noted that expressive talk or conversation "takes place against the background of a world that is silently taken for granted" (p. 152), but go on to emphasize that it is not a static world. Rather it is constantly changing, partly as a result of the very activity of keeping it in order:

> One may have doubts about one's religion; these doubts become real in a quite different way as one discusses them. One then "talks oneself into" these doubts; they are objectified as reality within one's own consciousness. Generally speaking, the conversational apparatus maintains reality by "talking through" various elements of experience and allocating them a definite place in the real world. (P. 153)

It is this talking through which is the heart of the expressive, and out of which the more differentiated forms of language discussed in this chapter eventually evolve. Yet it is not that one begins in the expressive and moves from it to the borders of the model outlined in figure 1; rather these other modes are added to the expressive, which continues to mature alongside of them.

Movement from one part of the model to another does not imply a shift in quality or maturity or value, though it does imply a shift in the manner of construing which the language itself demands. How the child comes to master these various modes, in particular those in the spectator role, will be our concern in the following chapters.

Three

A Sense of Story

Introduction

We have given the spectator role an important role in individual and cultural development, but clearly it is a role defined largely from the perspective of the adult looking back on earlier experience. This chapter will attempt to deepen that perspective by considering the spectator role as it appears to the child rather than the adult. We will be asking when the spectator role emerges as a separate part of language experience, how it is marked or distinguished by the child, and what specific sorts of expectations and presuppositions are developed about it. Our main examples will come from studies of children in London, England, and in New Haven, Connecticut, though the work of other investigators will be drawn on to support and broaden the base for our generalizations. Though the focus will be on the "sense of story" as a typical and central example,[1] it is the spectator role in general that is the real topic of what follows. The relationships between the specific illustration and the more general category should become clear in the course of our discussion.

Early Forms of the Spectator Role

Does spectator-role language exist at all for the very young child? Can we find any evidence of language use detached from the world of immediate action, times when the child is merely "playing" with words or using them to create what Langer (1953) has called a "virtual" world, a semblance of reality?[2] Many traditional theories of language development would certainly imply that such spectator-role uses would be a later acquisition, that language begins within a supporting social context without which it does not function, and that the earliest functions of language are interactive, even imative, rather than detached and personal in the ways characteristic of the spectator role.

Certain devices which later become part of the repertoire of poetic form correspond to very primitive, even prelanguage functions. Rhythm, for example, is an underlying physiological phenomenon of crucial importance in organizing ongoing life processes (cf. Langer 1967), and a close link between these body rhythms and the rhythms of language has often been noted. Vygotsky (1971) has attempted to use it to explain the pervasiveness of work songs and chants, and to see in them the Urforms out of which literary uses of language, detached from work, later develop. Chukovsky (1963) in Russia and White (1954) in New Zealand have also commented on the extent to which the young child responds to rhythm. Both have noted a trancelike fascination with verse that enthralls children even with adult poetry far above their level of comprehension. A child apparently expects to enjoy the rhythm itself, rather than to understand the words: a four-year-old's fascination with "Ode to a Grecian Urn" is one example which White has cited.

Presleep Monologues

More can be said about the origins of the spectator role, however, than simply that it will eventually incorporate processes present even in the infant. Our best approach is through Ruth Weir's discussions of *Language in the Crib* (1962). This study is based on the presleep monologues of Weir's son Anthony, recorded as he talked himself to sleep each night between his twenty-eighth and thirtieth months; roughly, at two-and-a-half. These monologues pose a basic challenge to traditional theories of language development, as George Miller notes in his introduction to the book: if language learning depends on a supporting environment responding to vocalizations, the monologues should never have taken place at all. They cannot be explained as perseveration, the reactivation of traces of language behavior "left over" from the child's daytime activities. On the contrary, they suggest (in Miller's words) "persistent, combinatorial play." As we shall see, they also provide us with our earliest examples of language in the spectator role.

Weir's discussions throw light on many aspects of the development of syntactic, morphological, and phonemic structures. For our present purposes, however, it is the larger units of discourse that are of most interest. It is with larger units—sequences ranging from several sentences to as many as twenty and thirty—that early forms of the spectator role are most evident. (Weir found that pause length could be used as a stable and consistent index to segment the monologues into sentence units; it is these divisions which are used in the examples which follow.) Although Anthony is alone while the recordings are being made, his monologues take the form of a social interchange. As he commands, chides, asks, and addresses a series of hypothetical companions, he is functioning happily in an imaginary world, creating his own version of Langer's (1953) "semblance of events lived and felt" (p. 212). This appears strikingly in the inventory of vocabulary, where the most frequent personalized noun is *Bobo,* the name of a toy which according to Weir had no special significance for Anthony other than its role as an audience. It was not particularly favored during daytime play, and was not missed when the family left for vacation without it. In the monologues, however, Bobo emerges again and again, in such contexts as "There's the white blanket, Bobo," "Look what Bobo did," and "Bobo night night."

Within this virtual social frame, Anthony develops several different uses of language in the spectator role. One centers on the sounds of language, which still present him with great difficulty. Words are, or can easily become, focal in his activities; their form and substance quite easily divert him. This produces sound play that to an adult, used to language functioning tacitly and transparently, seems highly sophisticated. One example which Weir presents in some detail is the phrase "Blanket like a lipstick." This represents a complex association between his mother's grooming habits and a corner of his blanket which Anthony spontaneously identified as his "blanket like a lipstick." According to Weir, this became a popular phrase in Anthony's daytime speech; it also appears regularly in the monologues. She argues, however, that in spite of the underlying semantic association, its function is not primarily referential. She breaks the phrase down into three units, each beginning with a strong stress, and diagrams "a striking pattern of interplay between stops and /l/":

blanket	bl	n kt
like a	l	k
lipstick	l p s t k	(P. 101)

Weir points out that the order of /l/ and /k/ is fixed in each
segment, with further play on the stopped consonants. The
first segment also repeats the vowel phoneme /E/, the third
segment the vowel phoneme /I/, giving further formal unity to
the structure as a whole.

As a single example, such structure could easily be dismissed
as fortuitous; it gains its strength from Weir's ability to multiply
such examples almost without end.[3] Some of the most interesting sequences involve an interplay between language-as-sound
and language-as-meaning, a process evident in the following
segment:

> ?oo
> ?oo
> ?oo
> ?oo
> ?oo
> Get shempoo
> Get shempoo
> Tryin
> Shampoo [repeated ten times]
> Shimming pool
> Shimming pool
> Shimming pool
> Want some water daddy
> (P. 170)

This begins with a relatively clear attempt to master a word that
has been giving difficulty; Anthony even acknowledges that he
is "tryin" to get it right. Eventually he manages, and confirms
his achievement with the ten repetitions of "shampoo." From
there he moves on to pure play, shifting from "shampoo" to
"shimming pool" with /sh/, /m/, /p/, and /oo/ all preserved
and in the same order. According to Weir, this is a word that
he does manage correctly in his daytime speech, confirming our
sense that the distortion is serving the formal pattern rather
than simply an error. But this word appears to strike up seman-

tic associations that bring Anthony back to the world of the present, and the demand for something to drink.

Finally, we should mention one of the clearest examples of sound play with no evident semantic content at all:

> Bink
> Let Bobo bink
> Bink ben bink
> Blue kink[4] (P. 105)

Ordering Experience

Anthony's concern with the substance of language is not the only "topic" to be found in the monologues. There are some which are just as clearly attempting to make sense of the nonlinguistic world of which he is a part. One of the longest sequences in the corpus, one discussed in some detail by Weir, seems to reflect the archetypal struggle for possession within a family. It is triggered off by "daddy" entering the room and then going out again; Anthony's speech returns again and again to the topic of "possession" and who belongs to whom. The sequence is very long and only part will be quoted here. It begins:

> That's for he
> Mamamama with Daddy
> Milk for Daddy
> Ok
> Daddy dance
> Daddy dance
> Hi Daddy
> Only Anthony
> Daddy dance
> Daddy dance
> Daddy give it
> Daddy not for Anthony
> No

This opening segment sets out the topics that recur throughout the full sequence. The obvious claim for the father in "That's for he" (a typical substitution for "me" in Anthony's speech); the conflict in his recognition that the attachment is shared, and probably not even equally; and the offering of milk, precious enough to the child, "for Daddy." "Daddy dance," according to Weir a rare phenomenon, seems to be a sound play, though it picks up some of the tonality of a refrain and appears again near the end of the series, helping to hold the whole together:

> Daddy put on a hat
> Daddy put on a coat
> Only Daddy can
> I put this in here
> See the doggie here
> See the doggie
> I see the doggie
> Kitty likes doggie
> Lights up here
> Daddy dance
> Daddy dance
> Daddy dance
> With Bobo
> What color's Bobo
> What color's Bobo
> (Pp. 138–39)

Weir traces a rondolike pattern throughout this monologue; there is a broad circular movement that brings the discussion back to topics like "Daddy dance" and "what color."

Such monologues give us a strong basis for claiming that the spectator role has already emerged by the age of two-and-a-half. The length of the monologues, the ease with which they are managed, and the obvious delight with which they are carried on makes us suspect that language used for looking on rather than participating in must begin even earlier, perhaps as early as the infant's first structured babbling. There are few demands on the language in these monologues, however; Anthony is alone and has no one but himself to please. The resulting language is very much in the expressive mode, with very little of what we would call poetic form, and little pressure toward articulation or reformulation of the construct system. But because they stem from a context free from external demands, the monologues leave open the question of whether children of this age can, when they want to, impose more form on their discourse.

Formal Characteristics of Stories

The stories which children tell, however, provide a direct approach to such questions. Though very young children may not be able to tell us in any full sense what they expect to find in a story, these expectations are reflected more or less directly in their attempts to tell stories to us. Pitcher and Prelinger (1963) have presented an extensive collection of such stories, gathered from middle-class American two- to five-year-olds in response to the question, "Tell me a story." Since the concerns of the original investigators were rather different from those in the present study, the corpus was reanalyzed as a source of information about the child's expectations about stories. (Procedures in the reanalyses of the 360 stories and further details about sampling are discussed in appendix 1.)

"Telling stories" is one of many uses of language in our culture, and has many conventions of language and usage associated with it. Willy (1975) has discussed many of these in the course of an analysis of 145 stories collected from six- and seven-year-old children. He points out that many of the stories read to young children are based on an earlier, oral tradition and are designed for a listening rather than a reading audience. Among the conventions noted by Willy and others (cf. Cazden 1972; Sacks 1972; Bettelheim 1976) are beginning with a title or formal opening phrase ("Once upon a time"), ending with a formal closing ("The end" or "happily ever after"), the use of a consistent past tense, a change of pitch or tone while storytelling, acceptance of "make-believe" characters and events, and the possibility of incorporating certain conventional or "stock" character types and situations. The extent to which these conventions are recognized and used by children can be taken, to a certain extent, as an indication of the degree to which stories have begun the long march from the child's initial recognition that a story is in some way different from other uses of language, to the final firmly established recognition of a story as a mode of communication, "an accepted technique for discussing the chances of life" (Harding 1962). Frye (1957) has emphasized the central role of conventions in literary experience, pointing out that the "problem of convention is the problem of how art can be communicable" (p. 99).

To explore this, the stories in the Pitcher and Prelinger collection were scored for the use of three such conventions: formal opening or title, formal closing, and consistent past tense. The results, summarized in detail in supplementary table 4, appendix 3, indicate that even the two-year-olds had begun to distinguish stories in these ways: 70 percent of them used at least one of these three devices. From two to five all three conventions showed a steady rise, till by five all but two of the stories analyzed (6.7 percent) were marked with at least one of these formal characteristics, and 47 percent were marked with all three. Statistically, the age changes for each of the three devices are highly significant; there are no significant differences in their use by boys and girls.

Two stories offered by Eliot, the first at two years and the second at five, illustrate the extremes of development with respect to these variables:

The daddy works in the bank. And Mommy cooks breakfast. Then we get up and get dressed. And the baby eats breakfast and honey. We go to the school and we get dressed like that. I put coat on and I go in the car. And the lion in the cage. The bear went so fast and he's going to bring the bear back, in the cage.

—Eliot M., 2 yr 11 mo (P. 31)

Once upon a time there were four cowboys. One was named Wilson, one was named Ashton, one was called Cheney. They all shot holdups and killed rattlesnakes and they ate them.

Then a storm came and lightening came but there wasn't a fire. One day in the woods another storm came and there were no lightening rods so the grass burned and their house burned up except they had a hose.

One day they got a dog and then in six days a wolf came and the dog got rabies. They shot the dog but before the wolf came a baby dog came out. One day the dog grew up like his father. They buried the dog and the wolf.

Then a bear came to their house. Their house was made of brick and the bear got in the door. And the cowboys were bigger than the bear. They were two feet. Then they killed the bear.

The cowboys lived in the jungle. A whole bunch of gorillas and lions and tigers came in their house. They were going to eat them up. They had a fight and every single one of the cowboys killed the gorillas and they lived happily ever after.

—Eliot M., 5 yr 1 mo (P. 121)

Many sorts of development have obviously taken place in the little over two years between these stories, but the point for the moment is the progress from no formal marking as a story with any of the three conventions studied here, to formal marking with all three. The first story is an expressive, almost transactional piece of writing, a report on events bound up closely in the world of the child. The second is clearly distinguished as a story, a poetic rather than a transactional form.

Fact and Fiction

The child's gradual mastery of the formal characteristics of a story is paralleled by a gradual development of understanding of conventions related to story content. The earliest interpretation seems to be that a story is something that happened in the past, a *history* rather than a fictional construct. This early interpretation is often accompanied by a belief in the immutability of stories—a faith which is eventually shaken by the recognition that behind each story there is a human author who has made it up. Still, it is a long time before a child begins to question the truth of stories, or even to wonder if the world of stories is "real" or "just a story." Something of this progression is evident in Dorothy White's (1954) diary chronicle of her daughter Carol's early experiences with stories. At two years eight months, Carol treated stories as inviolable, and quickly caught her mother up if words were changed: "hot buttered toast," for example, could not be interchanged with "afternoon tea" (p. 24), once Carol had heard the original version of the story. This aspect of a sense of story is long-lasting; during some preliminary work related to the present study we found it even in seven-year-olds asked how they might improve a story they had said they disliked. Most of the children misinterpreted the task and promptly named a different story that was already better; Stephen nominated *Sleeping Beauty* as a story he did not like:

> If you were telling *Sleeping Beauty,* could you change it so that you would like it?—*No.*—Why not?— ... —Is it alright to make changes in stories?—*No.*—Why not?— ... —Do you think you could make it better?—*No.*—Why not?—*Because you can't rub out the words.*
>
> —Stephen, 6 yr 9 mo
(Applebee 1973b)

Just after Carol's fourth birthday, she heard a poem which ended, "But I think/Mice are nice."

> "Who thinks?" Carol asked yesterday. "The man who wrote the poem," I answered. She looked at me questioningly but said no more.   (Pp. 100–101)

This sense of the poem as having an origin is closely tied to the question of its reality. Two months later, the issue appears in another diary entry:

> C (appearing suddenly before me in the bathroom): How do you make things?
> D: What things?
> C: Babies and poems and things like that?   (P.125)

Accompanying this general preoccupation with the origin of things was an emerging sense of the story as a *representation* of what it describes. Thus six days after the last incident:

> "What is this book *about?*" she asked. "Oh, a boy and a girl who go for a walk in England," I answered. She hunts round the pictures and puts her finger on the children, then, doubtfully, "This book's not *real* England!" "It's about England, Carol." "Yes, but not *real* England, just paper England." (P. 127)

This concern is a major step, but there is still a long way to go. It is another eight months before there is a diary entry noting that "Carol is now beginning to ask about 'true' and 'not true' stories. This is a new development [at almost five years]. Up till now everything has been accepted as real" (p. 188).

Nonsense

The progression toward the separation of fact and fiction, however, is not that simple and straightforward. From a very early age, certain kinds of stories are accepted and enjoyed precisely because they are *not* real; instead they invert the normal order of events in a way that the child recognizes and greets with laughter. The Russian children's poet Chukovsky has discussed this with respect to nonsense verse, which he treats as an important means of reality orientation. His point is much the one that we made in chapter two: to fully know one's reality, to be master of the world one has built for oneself, one must carry its principles through to the extremes. We must learn to recognize what is complete nonsense as well as what is complete sense. Such inversions, Chukovsky (1963) argues, are a major technical device in children's verse and in verse for children. Characters ride everything *but* a horse, sail in everything *but* a boat, live in everything *but* a house. This sort of reality confirmation through nonsense begins very early. Chukovsky noted it in his own daughter at twenty-three months, when she deliberately mixed up dogs and cats, "Oggie—meow"—at first uncertainly and then with great delight (pp. 97–98). Carlson and Anisfeld (1969), studying the speech of "Richard," found similar deliberate semantic deviations at twenty-two months, again in a context with spontaneous laughter. Such recognition of nonsense both depends on and reinforces a firmly based sense of what is real. If children feel an actual discrepancy between the facts and their need to order them, they will be distressed rather than amused. At three, Chukovsky's daughter began to cry when she heard that a cloud had "walked across the sky," for "How can a cloud possibly walk when it has no legs?" (p. 104).

Enjoyment of nonsense also appears in White's (1954) records, sometimes in contexts where it was never intended. Just past three-and-a-half, Carol begins to have trouble with *The Good Night Moon* by M.W. Brown:

When the text reads
Good night light
And the red balloon

Good night bears
And good night chairs.
Carol interrupted, "You don't say good night chairs."
Good night kittens,
Good night mittens.
"You don't say good night mittens." As I read on saying good
night to all the inanimate objects of the room, Carol began to
consider this a very good joke indeed, the smiles grew into
shrieks of laughter.   (P.73)

What is happening here is simple enough: Carol has just
learned the distinction between animate and inanimate, and
the story, albeit unintentionally, produces exactly the sort of
sense-in-nonsense, the "Aren't I smarter than they" delight
which Chukovsky has described.[5]

With the recognition of nonsense, "story" has become a more
complex concept for Carol, one that embraces both history and
nonsense; but she does not yet seem to recognize that fiction
rather than fact is one of the conventions of storytelling.

The question of the "truth" of stories is an important one in
the developmental course of the spectator role. As long as stories
are seen as true, or at least (as in nonsense) simply an inversion
of the true, they can only present the child with the world as it
is, a world to be assimilated and reconciled as best the child is
able. It is only after the story has emerged as a fiction that it
can begin a new journey toward a role in the exploration of
the world not as it is but as it might be, a world which poses
alternatives rather than declares certainties.

The Reality of the World of Stories

Yet if Carol White has begun to ask about fact and fiction by
the age of five, it will be several more years before most children
firmly expect stories to be something "made up" rather than
"real." As part of the present study, samples of six- and nine-
year-old London schoolchildren were asked a number of questions about this and related topics. Eighty-eight children were
interviewed in all, each child being assigned to one of two alter-
nate interview schedules. (Details of samples and procedures

are given in appendix 1.) Their responses, summarized in table 1, indicate that stories are astonishingly real even for six-year-olds who have had a year in a school environment where they hear stories at least daily. Heidi K. (6 yr 0 mo) is typically sure of her views:

Where does Cinderella live?—*With her two ugly sisters.*—Where is that?—*I think it's in an old house.*—Could we go for a visit?—(*No.*)—Why not?—*. . . Cause they'll say Cinderella can't come she'll have to wash up the plates and all the dishes and wash the floor.*—Hmm, do you think we could go visit the ugly sisters?—(*Yes.*)—We could? Where would we go?—*. . .*—Do you think it's near or far away?—*Far away.*

Later in the interview, she continued:

Is Cinderella a real person?—*Yes.*—What do you think she's doing right now?—*. . .*—What do you think she might be doing?—*Washing the floor.*—Are stories always about things that really happened?—*Yes.*—When did the things in *Little Red Riding Hood* happen?—*Don't know.*—When do you think they happened?—*September.* [It is September.]

Many are less quick to think that they could actually visit the characters they grant as real, posing one or another problem that would surely intervene. Distance is the most frequent obstacle, but there are many others. Thus Sarah L. (5 yr 9 mo), responding to the same questions:

Where does Cinderella live?—*In a castle.*—Where is the castle?—*Near the river.*—Could we go for a visit?—*No.*—Why not?—*You'd have to walk through the river.*—If we could get over the river, would she talk with us?—*Yes.*

Children's beliefs at this age are complex, however; they have not only the special problems of the story world to disentangle, but also questions of life and death, real and unreal in the world around them. Many shift their ground in the course of discussing such questions. Thus Kevin T. (6 yr 2 mo):

Where does Cinderella live?—*In the three woofs' house.*—The three wolves' place?—*Yeah.*—Where is that?—*I don't know.*—Do you think we could go and visit her if we knew where it

Table 1
Recognition of Fictional
Elements in Stories

Question	Children Showing Firm Recognition of Fiction (%)		
	Age 6 (n=22)	Age 9 (n=22)	Chi-square[a] (df=1)
Where does Cinderella live? Could we go for a visit?[b]	27.3%	86.4%	13.34***
Is Cinderella a real person? Was she ever a real person?	59.1	90.9	4.37*
Are stories always about things which really happened?	72.7	100.0	4.83**
Have you ever seen a giant?	59.1	95.5	6.34**
Overall rating at end of interview[c]	50.0	90.9	6.99***

[a] On tests of significance, see appendix 1. There were no significant differences between the sexes for any of these measures, using chi-square tests with ages pooled.

[b] Of those who recognize that Cinderella is not real, none of the nine-year-olds and 53.8 percent of the six-year-olds say she is a puppet or dolly; $p < .001$, two-tailed, using Fisher's exact test (Siegel 1956).

[c] Of those recognizing the fictional element, 18.2 percent of the six-year-olds and 95.0 percent of the nine-year-olds were rated as having a firm rather than a "wavering" opinion; $p < .001$, two-tailed, using chi-square with $df=1$.

* $p < .05$, one-tailed.
** $p < .01$, one-tailed.
*** $p < .005$, one-tailed.

was?—*No.*—Why not?—*Because it's a long way away.*—
[Later] Is Cinderella a real person?—*No.*—What is she?—
She's, she's, she's just a, just a dolly.—She's just a dolly? Now

what about her house? Do you think her house is a real house?—*No.*—Is it something we could go visit?—*No ... no I think there ain't such things as Cinderella.*—Where did we get the story about it from then?—*From the books.*—Aren't stories about things that really happened?—*No, some of them are.*

Kevin's "just a dolly" is one transitional form that appears quite frequently in these interviews (table 1, n. b); relegating characters to the status of long-dead but once-living is another. Joseph L. (6 yr 3 mo) has taken this tack:

Is Cinderella a real person?—*No.*—Was she ever a real person?—*Nope, she died.*—Did she used to be alive?—*Yes.*—When did she live?—*A long time ago, when I was one years old.*—Are stories always about things that really happened?—*Yes.*—When did the things in Little Red Riding Hood happen?—*A long time ago when I was a baby, they happened. There was witches and that, a long time ago. So when they started witch. . . they saw two good people and they made some more good people, so did the more horrible people. And they made more good people and the bad people got drowned.* —Are there still people like that?—*Nope, they were all killed, the police got them.*

Joseph's answer is interesting for its illustrations of a process which occurs again and again: the world of story is fully assimilated into the child's general view of the world, made sense of on the child's own terms. Here Noah and the flood have clearly helped to assimilate the concept of evil story characters, while the biblical story itself has been given its present-day avenging angels in the figure of the police. Joseph has evidently had a thorough exposure to the biblical narratives; they also provide him with a framework for discussing giants:

Have you ever seen a giant?—*David saw one when he was a little boy.*—Have you ever seen one?—*No.*—Why do you think you've never seen one?—*One was made, only David picked, . . .fired stones up and he fell to the ground and he was killed and he's in heaven.*—Do you think there ever used to be giants?—*Yes.*—Do you think there are any now?—*No, they were all killed by the police.*

Many of the children were familiar with the television series, *Land of the Giants,* and they almost inevitably declared that *those* giants, at least, were not real.[6] Colin C. (5 yr 11 mo) illustrates the perplexity many felt, a sense that some parts of the story world are fiction, while other parts just might be true:

> Have you ever seen a giant?—*No.*—Why do you think you've never seen one?—*Because, I've seen one on television, but that was a robot one, and that's a long way from here I know.* —Where do you think giants live?—*South America.*—Are giants real?—*(Yes.)*—They are? Do you think one will ever come here?—*But sometimes, I think, someone's inside driving it.*—Do you think a real giant will ever come here?—*Yah, I think that. And I always keep watch in my bedroom, cause I think ghosts come in and giants, and skeletons.*

By nine, such views have for the most part disappeared. Amanda is typical, interpreting the discussion as one about the events of the story itself:

> Where does Cinderella live?—[long pause] *I know she lives in a house with her two ugly sisters.*—Could we go there?—*NO!*— Why not?—*Because it isn't true!*

Even with older children, however, there are occasional reflections of the attitudes of their younger brothers and sisters. Thus Bruce B. (9 yr 7 mo) is quite consistent in his responses:

> Where does Cinderella live?—*In a palace.*—Where is the palace?—*Don't know.*—Do you think we could go visit her there?—*It's just like a cartoon.*—Could we go visit her there? —*Well that goes back in time. You need a time machine or something, could make you go there, so you couldn't.*— [Later] Have you ever seen a giant?—*We don't live when the giants was.*—Where do you think they live?—*Caves, up in the north, I mean in these hills.*—Were they real?—*I think so.*— Do you think there are any left now?—*No, died.*

Bruce remains very much in the minority at nine, with fewer than 10 percent of his peers persisting in such beliefs. But the fact that he is able to continue in this way, even if in a minority, is an important reflection of the role stories play. They remain very much a presentation of the world as it is or has been, and have not yet emerged as a mode to consider ways in which the world might be.[7]

Sources of Skepticism

The differing proportions of children who recognize the fictional element in stories when asked about specific characters or about the situation "in general" (table 1), suggest that six-year-olds begin to grasp that stories do not necessarily have to be about real things before they accept that the characters they have come to know well are part of this fictional world.[8] Most of the children were ambivalent, ready to declare with considerable determination that Cinderella is real, for example, and giants made up; others dismiss Cinderella as "just a puppet" and stoutly defend a more favored story friend. Edwina S. (6 yr 0 mo) had such a preference:

> Is Cinderella a real person?—(*No.*)—She isn't? What is she? —*Somebody dressed up in Cinderella's clothes.*—Is Snow White a real person?—(*Yes.*)—She is? Where do you think she lives?—*In her country.*—Could we go to visit her?—(*No.*) —Why not?—*Cause she lives in the country.*—Do you think that there might be a way to visit her sometime?—(*Yes.*)— What do you think she is doing right now?—*Washing up.*

Such exchanges, and there were many of them, suggest that there is no sudden realization that a story is "just a story," however much that has become the universal response by nine or ten. Instead, the characters shift slowly toward that special world of story, as each becomes more difficult to reconcile with the rest of the child's knowledge of the world. Edwina S., for example, knew enough about actors and actresses to realize that the television version she had seen was just about somebody dressed up in Cinderella's clothes, and that was enough to tip the balance of reality. The summary statistics which we have tabled do not reflect the extent to which the six-year-olds studied were uncertain in their beliefs, wavering about whether or not to accept the stories they knew as real. The overall rating given each child at the end of the interview has been dichotomized in table 1, but included categories for beliefs which seemed less than firm: these included 72.7 percent of the responses of the six-year-olds (and only 13.6 percent of those at nine). By six, though they will still defend the reality of some of the stories they know, doubts have begun to arise for most children.

The fact that even as late as six, many children are willing to defend the reality of stories has been noted by other investigators. Piaget (1929, p. 105) has commented briefly on it in his studies of Swiss children. Freidson (1953), working with American children, commented that five-year-olds "do not seem to use any criterion of reality" in discussing stories. Even by their third year in school, "we find most of the children accepting the stories if not as true events that directly effect them, then certainly not as 'just' stories." As one result, Freidson notes that their reactions are more intense than those of older children. In a more recent study, Harms (1972) similarly found that five-year-olds were still developing their concepts of fantasy and realism, while the seven- and nine-year-olds she studied had already done so.

Further Expectations about Story Characters

A child's sense of story also includes expectations about the behavior of various characters. The range here is very wide, with much of it overlapping the everyday world with which the child is also familiar: mommy and daddy appear in stories, as well as the Wizard of Oz and the Three Little Pigs. If our findings are accurate, most of these story characters become part of the "real world" which the young child is coming to master. Those which we as adults recognize as purely story characters are the beginning of what we might call the child's "literary" or "cultural" heritage, though the child does not recognize them as such; they are reference points which children share with one another and with the world of adults.[9] A child who plays the part of a story character, for example, is taking up a role whose possibilities have been defined by the story, and all of the children involved will understand, in an unconscious way, what those possibilities entail. This sort of assimilation extends even to linguistic structures which the child would otherwise find unnatural. White (1954) noticed such an instance with Carol at three years eight months:

> Tonight after tea I overheard Carol telling a story ... about the brief Sunday walk today. "There's a hospital. Sometimes a motor car came by and sometimes a truck. Sometimes a tram car came by and sometimes the people." She was following the phrasing and my exact intonation of voice when I had read the passage from *The Little White Gate,* "Sometimes a hedgehog came by and sometimes a mouse." (P. 76)

Richard, in Carlson and Anisfeld's (1969) study, similarly used songs or poems as frames for substitution, allowing him to produce utterances markedly longer than he could control in less structured speech situations.

Such experience with stories heard also overflows into the world of stories told. The reanalysis of the stories in the Pitcher and Prelinger (1963) collection, for example, found that the use of conventional story characters rose from 0 at two to 33.3 percent of the stories at five.[10] In the full set of 360 stories, Santa Claus was the most frequently named character, cowboys the most frequent conventional type, followed closely by witches, Indians, giants, and ghosts in declining order of frequency. The major characteristic of the use of these characters, however, was their diversity; even cowboys were used in only 17 of the 360 stories, Santa Claus in only 8.

Children gradually develop quite firm expectations about these story characters. Kuethe (1966), for example, found that in children's stories dogs tend to be associated with boys and cats with girls. And the children interviewed in London for the present study made a similar association. At six, some 46 percent expected a boy in a story to have a dog for a pet, and 32 percent expected a girl in a story to have a cat; both proportions rise significantly between six and nine, where they hover near 80 percent. The tendency for the boy's pet schema to be more firmly established than the girl's pet schema among the six-year-olds is interesting, in that it directly reflects Kuethe's findings: the stories he surveyed had boys with dogs more than twice as often as they had girls with cats.[11]

These figures are interesting but their interpretation is ambiguous; the pairings boy-dog and girl-cat are cultural and likely to be met in contexts other than stories. Results were similar, however, when children were asked what such characters as lions, wolves, rabbits, foxes, fairies, and witches are "usually like" in a story.[12] At six, 41 percent of the children had firmly developed expectations about the roles of at least half of the characters; by nine, this had risen to 86 percent of the children interviewed.

Jon M. at six years two months is typical of those who answered with "realistic" descriptions rather than with role evaluations:

> What is a lion in a story usually like?—*A big animal, with, ah, big teeth, ah, its got all fur around it.*—What is a wolf in a story usually like?—*It's a big animal with big sharp teeth, in the woods.*—What is a rabbit in a story usually like?— *It's white, it has little teeth, and ah it's got little black feet with fur on it.*—What is a fox in a story usually like?—*Ah, a little animal, with, ah, big ears and brown fur around it.*— What about a fairy?—*Ah, it's just a, like, it flies about, like a moth.*—What's a witch in a story usually like?—*Um, sometimes it flies around in a broomstick.*—What's she like?— *Horrible.*

Pressed about the witch, Jon moves on to reveal a fuller set of expectations, but certainly these characters are not yet identified primarily by the roles they play within a story context. Tina J. (5 yr 10 mo) has a much fuller set of expectations, though they are very much situation-bound, expressed as actions rather than in general terms:

> What is a lion in a story usually like?—*He always there, for, he always fight Tarzan.*—What is a wolf in a story usually like?—*A wolf like to eat big, big children or little children.*— What about a rabbit in a story?—*He eats carrots and things.* —How about a fox in a story?—*A fox eats big children or little children, ah, four or five or six or seven or two.*—What's a fairy like in a story?—*A fairy is a fairy mother . . .*—What does she do in a story? Turtles are usually very slow in a story, what are fairies like?—*Like a white thing, very pretty.*—How

about a witch?—*A witch very ugly, like he wouldn't be able to look like the yum yum.*

By nine, expectations about the roles which the various characters play had become much firmer. Nancy F.'s (9 yr 10 mo) response is one of the most fully developed, and also one of the briefest, in the whole sample:

What is a lion in a story usually like?—*Fierce.*—What about a wolf. What is a wolf in a story like?—*Hungry.*—What about a rabbit in a story?—*Fast.*—What about a fox in a story?—*Sly.*—What about a fairy?—*Kind.*—And a witch?—*Wicked.*

These characters include some met only in fantasy and others who are also part of the real world. Expectations in the two cases cannot be directly compared, since we lack a criterion for judging whether the roles assigned to different characters are in any sense representative of equivalent degrees of cultural consensus. The analysis was taken a bit further, however, by polling six adults in a seminar on language for their judgment of the "usual roles" each character plays in children's stories. Five of the six characters elicited equivalent constructs from at least five of the six adults: lions were seen as brave, rabbits as soft and cuddly, foxes as clever, fairies as good, and witches as evil. The five constructs on which the adults agreed were taken as defining role expectations of more or less equivalent strength, and the responses of the children were rescored as reflecting or not reflecting this adult expectation. With this approach, results were very different for characters met only in stories and those who are also a part of the real, nonstory world.[13] At six, 32 percent of the children expected a fairy to be good, 55 percent expected a witch to be bad, but none expected a lion to be brave, a rabbit to be cuddly, or a fox to be clever. By nine, there was very little change for foxes or rabbits (5 and 9 percent of the children, respectively, reflecting adult expectations), but lions were reported as brave by 32 percent, fairies as good by 86 percent, and witches as evil by everyone. (In making these tabulations, the adult expectation was treated as a superordinate construct subsuming a whole range of related constructs and actions; a witch turning people into toads, for example, was treated as reflecting the adult expectation of wickedness.) That children develop consistent expectations more rapidly for the fantasy characters is not surprising: a lion in a story and a lion in a zoo will build up conflicting expectations, whereas fairies and witches, restricted to the domain of fantasy, are able to build up a single, clear system of expectations more easily.

Such stock types provide these children with a set of expectations about characters whom they meet in stories. These expectations are purely conventional and culture-specific, though we would expect the process itself to be quite general. (For studies of cultural schemata in stories, see Blom et al. 1970; Beshai 1972; Helson 1973; and Sternglanz and Serbin 1974. Monson and Peltola [1976] list many similar studies.) In spite of Richards' (1929) protests about stock responses, such conventional symbols serve a useful purpose. Bettelheim (1976) has argued that the polarization of characters in children's literature enables the child "to comprehend easily the difference between the two, which he could not do as readily were the figures drawn more true to life, with all of the complexities that characterize real people. Ambiguities must wait until a relatively firm personality has been established" (p. 9). In the cases Bettelheim is discussing, the conventional expectations are used directly: witch and fairy, for example, will be posed against one another as villainess and heroine. In other stories these same expectations can be used in more subtle ways: the role of the cowardly lion in *The Wizard of Oz* is understandable only because we share an expectation that lions will be brave.

Summary

The available evidence carries us quite a way in considering the origin and early development of a child's sense of story. Anthony Weir's monologues give us reason to expect that spectator-role language begins very early for the child, quite likely as part of his earliest play with the sounds of language. By two-and-a-half, the earliest age at which we have many records, this use of language in the spectator role includes the shaping of experience as well as of language: both Anthony in his monologues and the children in the Pitcher and Prelinger (1963) collection use their language to discuss events of importance to them.

It is also clear that from a very early age these discussions begin to be subsumed within the conventional, culturally provided frame of the story mode; even the two-year-olds studied used at least some of the conventions studied in 70 percent of their stories. By five, they had begun to absorb common story characters into the stories they told, and by six, to explain their expectations about witches and fairies, lions and wolves. All of these expectations grow firmer with age, of course, as the child's experience with stories in particular and the spectator role in general increases.

More striking, perhaps, than these indications that the child begins quite early to make use of the conventions of the spectator role, is the marked failure to separate spectator-role experience from more direct experiences with the world. Whereas the adult, and even the nine-year-old, recognizes that stories are "just make-believe," children as old as six, with a full year in school, are less dismissive. Some 73 percent of those studied remained uncertain about whether story characters and events are real; 50 percent tended to think they probably are. Though children apparently recognize nonsense at quite an early age, they treat this as a simple inversion of the real rather than as something "made up" in the adult sense. Children preserve their stories in lands far away and times long ago before they finally surrender to the skepticism of their peers.

This lack of differentiation between fact and fiction makes the spectator role a powerful mode for extending the relatively limited experience of young children. The stories they hear help them to acquire expectations about what the world is like—its vocabulary and syntax as well as its people and places—without the distracting pressure of separating the real from the make-believe. And though they will eventually learn that some of this world is only fiction, it is specific characters and specific events which will be rejected; the recurrent patterns of values, the stable expectations about the roles and relationships which are part of their culture, will remain. It is these underlying patterns, not the witches and giants which give them their concrete form, which make stories an important agent of socialization, one of many modes through which the young are taught the values and standards of their elders.

Four

Narrative Form

Introduction

Spectator-role language relies on what we have called poetic form—systems of relationships among the constituent parts of a work. While the logical structure of transactional language has been quite fully explored, the structure underlying poetic form has been relatively intractable. The simplicity of the stories children tell, however, helps to highlight the principles which underlie their form. Our investigations will, in fact, suggest two processes—centering and chaining—which are not only basic to the narrative structure of children's stories, but also major constituents of poetic form in more sophisticated, adult works.

Organization and Complexity in Children's Stories
Age Changes in Complexity

The complexity of a task is in part a function of the number of elements which must be controlled or coordinated. Such task complexity seems an important and obvious dimension of developmental change; we would expect that the elements which go into a story would grow more complex with age on virtually any measure of complexity we chose to use. This is certainly true of the stories in the Pitcher and Prelinger (1963) collection: number of words, number of T-units, number of characters, number of incidents, and the average number of words per T-unit all show a consistent and significant rise with age, whether considered individually or as a set.[1] Such findings are not surprising and would be consistent with almost any view of the developmental processes. They provide, however, the introduction to the next question we want to ask, How do children organize the complexity in the stories they tell?

An Approach through Theories of Concept Development

Complexity in most areas of cognition is handled through the imposition of structure, and stories are no exception. Studies by

Brown (1958), Vygotsky (1962), Bruner et al. (1956, 1966), and others have illustrated the differing ways in which attributes may be structured in defining category membership or in elaborating a new concept. If we treat the plots of stories as a series of elements or incidents, each of which has a series of attributes (characters, actions, settings, themes), we can use this previous work in concept development to provide a highly suggestive model for our analysis of narrative form. In the stories told by children between two and five, six basic types of structures were found, bearing a remarkable resemblance to Vygotsky's (1962) stages in concept development and showing the same general developmental order. Figure 2 provides a schematic summary of these structures, each of which will be described in the present chapter. Nine types were originally defined on the basis of an analysis of stories not in the main sample; these categories were later collapsed to the six presented in detail after the most mature and least mature forms were found to occur rarely within the sample.

Heaps

Vygotsky (1962) was able to specify a series of stages in concept development after close analysis of an experiment in which children were asked to master the concepts used to label (with nonsense words) a collection of blocks representing a variety of colors and shapes. (In this set, the word *lag* stood for tall large figures, *bik* for flat large figures, and so on.) He labeled the first general stage "heaps," from the tendency of the child simply to reach out and heap the blocks up when asked to show which ones went together. As Vygotsky described it, the heap is a method of solving a problem that adults would solve by using a concept, and reveals "a diffuse, undirected extension of the meaning of the sign (artificial word) to inherently unrelated objects linked by chance in the child's perception" (p. 59). In narrative form, of course, we have no sign for the category (except in some cases a title), but we nonetheless have a conceptual "whole" to organize. With Vygotsky's heap this organization is syncretistic, rooted in the child's perception and

Figure 2

The structure of children's stories. Arrows indicate complementary attributes; straight lines, shared attributes; parallelograms, centers; circles, incidents or elements.

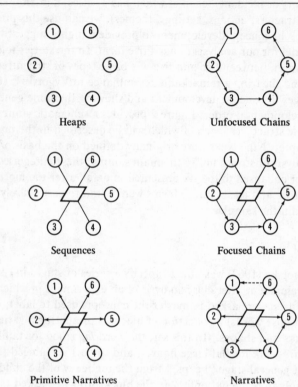

Heaps

Unfocused Chains

Sequences

Focused Chains

Primitive Narratives

Narratives

essentially unrelated to the characteristics of the material to be organized. This situation has a clear parallel in the stories children tell:

A girl and a boy, and a mother and maybe a daddy. And then a piggy. And then a horse. And maybe a cow. And a chair. And food. And a car. Maybe a painting. Maybe a baby. Maybe a mountain stone, somebody threw a stone on a bear, and the bear's head broke right off. A big stone, this big [holds out arms]. And they didn't have glue either. They had to buy some at the store. You can't buy some in the morning. Tomorrow morning they're gonna buy some. Glue his head on. And the baby bear will look at a book.

> —Warren P., 3 yr 7 mo
> (Pp. 53–54)

The daddy works in the bank. And Mommy cooks breakfast. Then we get up and get dressed. And the baby eats breakfast and honey. We go to the school and we get dressed like that. I put coat on and I go in the car. And the lion in the cage. The bear went so fast and he's going to bring the bear back, in the cage.

> —Eliot M., 2 yr 11 mo (P. 31)

Eliot's organization is virtually that of immediate perception, with few links from one sentence to another. Warren's begins equally syncretistically, with an almost free-association list of characters, but it does take on further form in the last few lines. This is important to note, for it is a general characteristic of children's stories: modes of organization emerge clearly, but many stories use more than one method of organization in the course of their narrative. The heap is a very primitive mode of organization; even at two, it was used by only one-sixth of the children in the Pitcher and Prelinger (1963) sample (see table 2).

In the first of many parallels that will be evident with adult literature, Smith (1968), in her analysis of the structure of poetry, notes that the sophisticated poet will sometimes use a similar associative structure. The difference is that the adult form "is controlled at every point by its ultimately expressive design" (p. 141), and represents a choice by the poet from among many available structures. For the very young child, on the other hand, it may be the only structure available.

Sequences

Vygotsky's second major phase of concept development is what he calls thinking in complexes. Unlike heaps, complexes show actual bonds between objects being grouped together but (unlike true concepts) the bonds are *"concrete and factual* rather than abstract and logical" (p. 61). Vygotsky breaks complexes down

Table 2   The Structure of Children's
                               Stories[a]

| | No. of Stories | | | | |
Plot Structure	Age 2 (n=30)	Age 3 (n=30)	Age 4 (n=30)	Age 5 (n=30)	Total (n=120)
Heaps	5	3	0	2	10
Sequences	13	6	7	1	27
Primitive narratives	7	7	3	0	17
Unfocused chains	0	2	3	5	10
Focused chains	5	11	16	16	48
Narratives	0	1	1	6	8

[a]Chi-square for age (ages two and three versus ages four and five) $= 28.63$, $df = 5$, $p < .001$, two-tailed. Chi-square for sex $= 1.47$, $df = 5$, *ns*. On tests of significance, see appendix 1.

into a number of stages which have parallels in the organization of children's stories.

The first of these is the associative complex. Its basic form is a nucleus to which other objects are linked on the basis of concrete similarities, though the shared attribute may change from one link to another. With the blocks, for example, if the first chosen is a small red triangle, the child may later add a small block, a red block, and a triangular block, each linked to the nucleus on the basis of one shared attribute. In telling stories, young children similarly make use of *sequences* in which the events have a superficial sequence in time, but this sequence is arbitrary. Event A is said to happen after event B, without any discernible causal link between them. Instead, the events are linked together on the basis of an attribute shared with a common *center* or core of the story. This center can take a number of different forms: it may be a certain kind of action repeated over and over, a certain kind of character (for example, a bad man), or sometimes a "scene" or situation (in Burke's [1945] sense) such as "the events of the day." In a sequence, the associations between the incidents and their center are limited to bonds of *similarity* rather than causality or complementarity;

though the story can grow longer, it cannot develop in new directions. The structure remains too weak to amplify the core around which the story is built, to explore or clarify the situation in any very productive sense. Still, the process of centering which appears here in this limited form is a powerful one that emerges again as part of more sophisticated plot structures.

The following stories illustrate some of the forms a sequence can take:

Little boy played. He cried. He's all right. He went home. He went to bed. When he wakes up you're gonna say good-night to him.
—Daniel W., 2 yr 10 mo
(Pp. 30–31)

A doggie and he said "go out." And then Mommy take him in. Then the next day he went to sleep. All waked up and started to cry. All go to get dinner. Then we go to Cheshire. And we all sleep all by ourselves in the little bed.
—Tricia W., 3 yr 10 mo
(P. 69)

A fierce poisonous snake and he ate a monster. And then he telephoned on the telephone. He went to someone's house and he ate some dog dirty. He went in someone's car and ate the seat off. Then he ate some bushes. Then he went some stairs and ate some stair meat. Then he ate himself.
—Larry W., 4 yr 3 mo (P. 85)

The two major forms underlying these stories seem to be (1) A does X, A does Y, and A does Z; and (2) A does X to N, A does X to O, and A does X to P. Daniel's and Tricia's stories represent the first of these patterns, though Tricia shifts partway through from "doggie" to "we" as the constant center. Larry's represents the second pattern, rarer in this sample and perhaps developmentally more advanced. Such sequences are the most frequent structure in the stories from the two-year-olds, and continue in about 20 percent of the stories at three and four (table 2). In a more controlled form, they have their counterparts in the catalogs and "paratactic" structures discussed by Smith (1968, pp. 98ff.). They also occur frequently as an organizational principle in nursery rhymes, lullabies, and folk songs which have an almost infinitely expandable number of verses.[2]

Primitive Narrative

Vygotsky's second phase of thinking in complexes involves what he calls "collections." Here the structure is based on complementarity rather than similarity; objects are grouped together to form a set, as, for example, a knife, fork, and spoon form a set of dinner implements. Vygotsky notes that this kind of complex is deeply rooted in practical experience; though we can create a superordinate construct (for example, "dinner implements") to describe the result, the basis for the child is still concrete, based in their mutual participation in the same practical operation, their functional cooperation in a given situation. When children use this mode of organization in telling their stories, it results in *primitive narratives,* each of which has a concrete core or center —an object or event that has temporarily assumed some importance to the child—which is then developed by collecting around it a set of complementary attributes. Instead of a bad character leading to another bad character as happens in sequences, with primitive narratives a bad character is more likely to lead to a spanking, one of the complementary, situationally related implications of "being bad" in the child's world. The stories that develop from this type of structure are sometimes quite well formed; the concrete core serves to give them a point or focus which the collection around it amplifies and clarifies. The situation by the end of the story has been in a real sense better understood. This form of narrative structure occurred in about 20 percent of the stories of the two- and three-year-olds, and 10 percent of those at four (table 2). Though we have no direct evidence, one would suspect that this is the major way in which children assimilate the stories they hear: as a collection of complementary events organized around a central situation or concrete core.

With the stories children tell, this remains a primitive form in that its center and its amplifications are concrete rather than conceptual, with the links among them those that have been

forged by shared situations. The form that results is in one sense
fortuitous, a reading back by the adult of more than the child
put in. Trudy's story of Sugar Bear illustrates how well formed
some of the stories can be:

> Sugar Bear is so funny and furry. Sometimes when they go to
> parties at night, I put dresses on him. When I look at him, he
> has his face so mad. I got him for Christmas, and his face was
> so mad. And when my animals are bad, we made a stock, and
> we put them in a stock. They run and jump in the house and
> they shouldn't do it at all, 'cause the people downstairs don't
> like it. She 'plains about that noise. I spank the bears. I don't
> like them to be bad anymore.
>
> —Trudy B., 3 yr 3 mo
> (Pp. 69–70)

Lucetta's and Kenneth's stories, on the other hand, do not have
the same sort of control; yet still a concrete nucleus is clear
in both:

> A little girl drawed her mommy. Then the mommy got mad at
> her and she cried. She lost her mommy's cookies. She got
> mad at her again. And she drawed her mommy again. And
> her mommy got mad at her again. And her daddy got home.
> That was Judy.
>
> —Lucetta D., 3 yr 4 mo
> (P. 62)

> The little boy dropped the ink. It broke. He cried. He cried
> some more. His mommy fixed it for him. He went to bed with
> it. The bottle didn't fall out and break. It was tied on to a
> string. He played with it.
>
> —Kenneth A., 2 yr 10 mo
> (P. 32)

Unfocused Chain

The next type of complex which Vygotsky describes is the chain
complex. Here each element shares a clear concrete attribute
with the next, but this defining attribute is constantly shifting;
the result is a chain in which the head bears very little relation to
the tail. In organizing the blocks, for example, a child may

begin with a red triangle, add another triangle which happens to be green, and add to that another green block which happens to be square. In the children's stories, there is a corresponding set of *unfocused chain narratives.* Here the incidents lead quite directly from one to another, but the attributes which link them continue to shift—characters pass in and out of the story, the type of action changes, the setting blurs. The result is a story which, taking its incidents in pairs, has much of the structure of a narrative, but which as a whole loses its point and direction. Thea's (5 yr 0 mo) is one good example:

> A wildcat. Then a horse came. Then they had a fight. Then the wildcat was dead. Then the horse went off. Then he met another horse. It was a lady horse. Then they lived with each other. Then another wildcat came. He was the father of the wildcats. He fired up the father horse and he was dead. Then the mother wildcat came and the father wildcat took the horse home with him. Then they eated him up. The mother was crying. Then she found another father. Then she washed the clothes. Then a donkey came along. Then the mother was afraid to go there where her washing was done. The donkey married the horse.
>
> —Thea M., 5 yr 0 mo
> (Pp. 148–49)

The amount of material managed in a story such as this can be quite large, but the lack of a center or "point" prevents it from becoming a structured whole in which the various parts can all be related to one another. Though unfocused chains are relatively rare, rising to about 16 percent of the stories analyzed at five, they are important as the first example of the use of chaining as an underlying structural device.

Focused Chain

Vygotsky has argued that before true concepts emerge, children make use of pseudoconcepts which are superficially similar but which remain perceptually rather than conceptually based. With the blocks, yellow triangles may be grouped together not because of an abstract notion of "yellow triangle," but because of the concrete perceptual associations among the members of the set. Vygotsky's blocks do not allow much amplification of this pseudoconcept, but in the children's stories there is a clear stage in which the processes of chaining and of centering around concrete attributes are joined within one narrative. In its most typical form, the center is a main character who goes through a series of events linked one to another just as in the unfocused chain. This produces a *focused chain narrative* of the "continuing adventures of..." type. (It is quite common in such adult genres as radio serials and adventure stories, as well as in children's tales.[3]) The organization remains pseudoconceptual rather than conceptual, however, in that the center is rooted in the concrete. Kip's tale of Davy Crockett is typical of the sort of story that results:

> Davy Crockett he was walking in the woods, then he swimmed in the water to get to the other side. Then there was a boat that picked him up. Then he got to the other side. He went into the woods. He was in the place where Indians made. The Indians came and got him. Then pretty soon he got loose. The Indians let him loose.
>
> —Kip P., 4 yr 9 mo (P. 83)

This is the most popular type of narrative structure among the older children, accounting for over half of the stories at five.

Narratives

The last major method of organization evident in the children's stories seems to result from an expansion of the centering of the focused chain to include links based on complementary attributes—a shift similar to that between sequences and primitive narratives at an earlier stage (see fig. 2). The effect of this is to allow the center or situation around which the story is built to be developed over the course of the narrative, much as the situation in the primitive narrative could be elaborated and clarified. Each incident not only develops out of the previous one, but at the same time elaborates a new aspect of the theme or situation. Such stories seem to have a consistent forward movement and often, though not necessarily, a climax at the end. Kirk's story of the "silly dog" who runs away, gets in trouble, and learns his lesson is a good example of the general form:

> Once there was a doggy and a little boy. This doggy was pretty silly. He ran away from the little boy and went farther and farther away. The little boy caught the doggy. He reached out and caught the little doggy with his hands. He put the doggy down. The doggy ran away again. He came near a railroad track. He stepped on it and the train ran over him. But he was still alive. This was a big white bull dog and he wanted to go back to his home. When the little boy went back home he found the doggy. He was happy. His doggy was still alive.
>
> —Kirk W., 4 yr 10 mo (P. 83)

In such stories, the core which holds everything together can rely either on concrete, perceptual bonds or on abstract, conceptual ones. In the latter case, the structure seems to correspond to what Vygotsky designates as "true concepts"; this is the stage at which stories begin to have a theme or moral. Tracy's story of Johnny Hong Kong is closer to this than any of the others in the whole collection:

> There was a boy named Johnny Hong Kong and finally he grew up and went to school and after that all he ever did was sit all day and think. He hardly even went to the bathroom. And he thought every day and every thought he thought up his head got bigger and bigger. One day it got so big he had to go live up in the attic with trunks and winter clothes. So his mother bought some gold fish and let them live in his head— he swallowed them—and every time he thought, a fish would eat it up until he was even so he never thought again, and he felt much better.
>
> —Tracy H., 5 yr 8 mo (P. 133)

With a somewhat older group of children, it might be useful to try to untangle stories such as this from others in which the theme or center is less abstract, but the frequency of both sorts was low enough to make such a distinction unprofitable with these two- to five-year-olds. In any event, the use of this type of organization increased sharply with age, from none at age two to 20 percent of the sample at age five—still of course only a small percentage, but nonetheless a major shift.

Sharpening Category Definitions

As we noted before, many stories do not fit neatly into one or another of the six categories, showing different types of narrative structure in different sections. For the present study, judgments were made globally, on the basis of the predominant mode of organization. (On rating procedures and reliabilities, see appendix 1.) The sensitivity of the analysis might be improved by allowing transitional categorizations for stories which show clear shifts. It is also possible that, retrospectively, the category definitions could be sharpened by specifying more precisely the nature of the defining attributes for each narrative structure. Primitive narrative, for example, might be limited to stories in which character and setting are both held constant, as they were for the majority but not the totality of stories in the present analysis. (This and other detailed characteristics are summarized in supplementary table 7, appendix 3.) A multiple discriminant function analysis was undertaken to further explore the categories derived for the present study. It indicated that the worst overlap occurred between sequences and focused chains, and between focused chains and primitive narrative; these statistical results correspond to the general impression of the raters in scoring the stories.[4] Any further analyses along the lines of this series should begin by formulating the defining differences between these pairs more precisely.

Plot Structure and Task Complexity

Our analysis of the conceptual organization of these stories began with the argument that we would be looking at ways in which the children manage complexity. So far we have demonstrated that the structurally more mature forms, using Vygotsky's findings about developmental sequence, are more prevalent at the older ages and, separately, that the stories told by older children are more complex. We have not shown that the relationship between the two developments is more than a fortuitous by-product of a mutual relationship with age. To explore this further, a multivariate analysis of covariance was carried out on differences in complexity among the major plot structures, after controlling for age. This analysis asks in effect if age alone is enough to explain the changes in the other variables, or if plot structure as well as age is related to the complexity of the stories. The five simple measures of complexity discussed earlier were used in this analysis, and resulted in two significant dimensions of difference among the plot forms. The first and larger of these reflected differences in the average number of characters included in the various plot forms; the second was a general effect to which all measures of complexity except the number of incidents contributed.[5]

What these results suggest is that there are real differences in the complexity of the stories corresponding to the different methods of structuring the plots, differences which remain even after allowing for the fact that certain plot structures are used mostly by the older children in this sample. This is a much more interesting finding than that of age changes in complexity and in plot structure separately considered.

Yet the succession of ways of organizing a story bears a complex relationship to the overall complexity of the comprehension and production task facing the child. Looking only at the modes of organization, each stage is more complex than the previous one, and is correspondingly more difficult to master. (Hence the fact that they are not all immediately available to the two-year-old.) The heap, like all forms of syncretistic thought, creates the least complex task: the child has no links among the parts of the story to control, simply taking each event singly as it comes to his or her attention. The sequence is more complex in that the child must keep the core or center constant, so that other elements can be linked to it on the basis of perceived similarity. This added structural complication, however, simultaneously simplifies the task of organizing a larger set of elements; it provides a model or set of expectations about the form that each new segment of the story will take. In Larry W.'s story quoted above, for example, everything that comes in is going to be eaten, and that is all there is to it! In moving from the sequence to the primitive narrative, the child adds the complexity of dealing with bonds of complementarity as well as similarity, but this again simplifies the problem of dealing with an expanding number of distinct story elements. For in this version (and for the first time), there is a sense in which the parts which belong to the story are entailed within the initial situation. Whereas Larry W.'s story structure gives him no basis for predicting *what* will be eaten, Trudy B.'s comments about Sugar Bear are all based in expectations which derive from her experiences with the bear; she should have a better chance of reconstructing the story if asked to tell it again.

The move from primitive narrative built around centering to chain narrative seems to be one of a greater order of magnitude than the previous shifts. Rather than singling out one attribute similar to or complementary with the organizing core, the child becomes aware of the multitude of attributes associated with each new incident in the story, letting the next incident develop out of the most recent addition rather than returning to the constant center. This breaks the syncretistic tendency to focus on a single aspect of each new incident and replaces it with a fuller awareness of the evolving possibilities of the situation being depicted. This added structural complexity once again simplifies the task of bringing ever-larger numbers of elements into the story: the amount of amplification that can take place around a single center is obviously limited in a way that amplification around each new incident added to the story is not. The chain maintains the advantage of the primitive narrative in allowing events to evolve out of one another, but by shifting the focus to each new link of the chain it simultaneously broadens almost indefinitely the possible scope.

The unfocused chain narrative presents the child with a new problem, analogous to that faced earlier with the sequence: because the structure lacks a focus or center, there is no control over what aspect of the situation will be elaborated. The next stage, the focused chain, improves on that by giving one aspect of the situation, usually a character, a central role; by holding this constant, the story begins to be "fixed" again, to be nearly reconstructable. Finally, when the story moves to the last stage dealt with here, the true narrative, its plot has in a sense become reversible: the ending is entailed within the initial situation. At this stage the incidents are linked both by centering and by chaining and are thus more fully controlled. Both the teller and listener are likely to know more about what comes next than with any of the earlier forms.[6]

Further Development of Poetic Form

The simple narratives in this collection of stories do not represent the final stage of development in literary structure, but the patterns which are traced here are arguably the ones out of which even more complex structures will be built. The two basic mechanisms are centering and chaining, each of which is a way in which one element in a discourse can be linked to another. With chaining, elements are joined on the basis of links of complementarity or similarity, one to another. In children's stories, the linking elements usually involve time sequence and causality, but in other spectator-role forms we might expect to find other sorts of chains—of images, say, or ideas or even sounds. With centering, on the other hand, each new element is linked to one special aspect (for example, character, theme, setting) which is held constant throughout the story. This gives unity and focus, insuring that there will be an overall "shape" as well as links between incidents taken in pairs.

Once a narrative has the structure we have called true narrative, it has reached a point where it can itself become an element to be bound, by chaining or centering, within a structure that is more complex still. It can become an episode or incident within a larger whole. This process was already evident in a few of the selections in the Pitcher and Prelinger (1963) collection. Consider, for example, Frances B.'s (5 yr 0 mo) contribution:

> Once upon a time there is a rabbit up a tree. And a boy got a fishing net. "May I stay for dinner for a few nights because I have no place to live? When I go away, I'm going to George Washington."
> He put the fishing net back in the rabbit's hole when he had dinner. There was a boy walking over to his house; he was sad. Here comes the rabbit to let the poor sad boy down the ladder into his house. "And after I visit you I am going back to my house in New York," the boys said this.

In the woods one girl was walking; she was very happy. She wanted a place to live. Her mother and her baby had died so she wanted a place to live. So she and her daddy packed up her things. They went to live with the boy and the rabbit and they were all happy all together in the old little house.

And they all turned to be rabbits because they didn't eat regular food; they ate carrots and the mother rabbit read stories to them all. And the mother rabbit let the girl and daddy down the ladder; the suitcase was heavy. The mother rabbit showed them a room and said they could stay forever. (Pp. 138–39)

The structure here is quite simple, but it has begun to break up into two separate incidents each with its own individual focus (one on the boy with no place to go, the other on the girl whose mother has died), and an overall center in the problem of loss and separation. In adult literature, the way in which these processes are combined defines the amount of narrative form with which we are willing to credit a work. A diary or memoir, for example, which remains quite close to the expressive, usually takes its structure from simple sequence. Here the narrator is the aspect of the story which remains constant throughout, but beyond this there is little overall unity. The relationship between one episode and the next tends to be a matter of time sequence, even though some of the episodes may be long-lasting and highly structured in themselves. In an adventure story—James Bond, say—there is somewhat more form, with the character still being held constant but the incidents also being closely chained together, each motivating the next. The extent to which there is any further centering in such stories varies greatly; in a Sherlock Holmes adventure there is a strong forward movement, progress toward the goal of solving the mystery; in a James Bond book there is much less of this, with more focus on the excitement generated by each incident and new danger in itself.

Finally when we move to fully poetic forms, both chaining and centering become all-pervasive. In a play such as *King Lear,* for example, it matters little whether the element we choose for analysis is the word, the line, the incident, the scene, the act, the character, the image, or the symbol; at each level such elements are bound in complex relationships one to another, and have an overall center or point as well. Cordelia's character, for example, emerges for us out of her separate actions throughout the play; these actions have one center which involves the type of character she is. At the same time, this type is itself part of a complementary set of possible types represented by Cordelia and her sisters. It is precisely because the full set of centerings and chainings in a fully developed poetic form are so complex that the task of the literary critic is so difficult, the rewards for the reader so rich. And it is also because these relationships are so complex, with each aspect simultaneously part of so many different chains and centers, organized at so many different levels in the structural hierarchy, that the full response to a poetic form cannot be a transactional, analytic one but must be the complex, assimilative, personal formulation that comes only in the spectator role.

Summary

Analysis of the stories children tell has considerably increased our understanding of poetic form, both in its developmental and its later, more sophisticated stages. From the perspective that has emerged here, there is an interplay between form and content in which increasingly complex material is dealt with through the expedient of organizing it more thoroughly. By approaching the plots of the children's stories as conceptual structures or modes of organization, it has been possible to recognize a series of stages parallel to those which Vygotsky (1962) has described for concept development in general. From least to most complex, the six major stages of narrative form found here are heaps, sequences, primitive narratives, unfocused chains, focused chains, and true narratives. Each in turn represents a progressively more complex combination of two basic structuring principles, centering and chaining. By recognizing that these can apply recursively to ever-larger units of discourse, they can be seen to underlie adult uses of language in the spectator role, as well as the children's uses from which they were derived.

Five

Fantasy
and Distancing

Introduction

If poetic form reflects structure or organization imposed on experience, the experiences with which children deal in their stories also show some interesting developmental shifts in the amount of fantasy which they employ. Fantasy as it will be treated here is primarily an aspect of the content rather than of the form of a work, but it too is a resource at the disposal of the storyteller to use or not as he or she sees fit. Developmental changes in these resources and in the contexts in which they are used will be our topic in this chapter.

The Widening Realm of the Possible

Witches and fairies, Santa Claus and Cinderella—a child's familiarity with such characters represents a widening view of the world, an extension of the boundaries away from the self toward an unknown horizon. From this point of view, fantasy is not so much the "fantastical" as it is part of a continuum that begins in the world of immediate experience, passes outward toward distant lands, and outward again into purely imaginative realms. Each step along this continuum increases the complexity of the child's world by admitting new elements into it; and, as we might expect, these elements are only gradually accepted and mastered.

Carol White, for example, begins with an interest only in things she already knows, and she uses those things to help her make sense of the unfamiliar. White (1954) recounts Carol's problems at two years five months with a story about "lions":

> Carol was more than puzzled by the lions. "Clothes-lions" is her usual pronunciation, and she looked for pegs and washing in the picture. Kangaroos baffled her too, but gradually, because these exotic animals were embedded among more familiar things, she came to accept them and give them their names. (P. 11)

There is a very close interaction between Carol's world of stories and that of her life, each set of experiences helping her to understand the other. With the "clothes-lions," Carol uses her everyday world to try to make sense of the book she is reading; a few weeks later there is a striking illustration of the opposite sort of movement. This occurs when Carol has her first venture out of the house at night, an experience which terrifies her until she remembers the dark night in one of her books; then all is well. The story gives her a pattern of expectations which allows her to make sense of the darkness she finds (p. 16).

The sort of familiarity which a child demands in a story is often a social one, a doing of things which the child expects to have done. Thus *Peter Rabbit* is a manageable story for Carol at two years eight months because of its familiar family setting (p. 26). Carol gradually begins to enjoy stories set more distantly, until by four years three months White is commenting:

> The background of the story is foreign and strange, but the four-year-old seems excited by things because they are strange. In contrast to the two-year-old who is most interested in what is most familiar, four years responds to what is less familiar. One can read a story about remote places now to Carol as long as the pictures make the reality quite clear. The illustrations must confirm the text; the two together, words and pictures, can take the child far beyond her immediate experience. (P. 139)

Carol's interests, then, show a considerable shift from two to five in the extent to which a story can be about worlds beyond her own. A similar progression is evident in the stories in the Pitcher and Prelinger (1963) collection. At the age of two, these stories remain very close to the world of the child's immediate experience. Bernice's is typical, both in its familiar family setting and in the way animal characters are casually assimilated to this everyday world:

> Once there was an elephant. The mommy fixed his breakfast. Then he played with his toys. Then he drank his milk. The doggie came into his house. And I had to chase him away. The milkman came. The doggie jumped on the milkman. Then the milkman "sweetied" the doggie on his back. Then the doggie went away.
>
> —Bernice W., 2 yr 11 mo
> (P. 35)

At two, 97 percent of the stories had settings that were realistic in the sense of being tied to the world the child would know—almost always the home and its immediate surroundings. Some 77 percent depicted actions that were appropriate within this world, and in 70 percent the actions were carried out by similarly realistic characters.[1] Ten percent of the children involved themselves directly in the action, as Bernice did in her story.

By five, the world explored in stories had shifted away from this personal center. Only 7 percent of the stories analyzed remained concerned with actions the child is likely to have experienced; 33 percent were set in the child's immediate world; and 37 percent involved realistic characters. Across all four ages, there was a gradual shift from completely realistic to intermediately distanced and finally to purely fantasy worlds. Age changes in all three of these aspects of fantasy, and for the three taken as a set, are highly significant (see supplementary table 8, appendix 3).

When fantasy is viewed in this way, there is a tendency in the stories analyzed for girls to tell more realistic stories than boys, but this may result from an interaction between our definition of fantasy and cultural stereotypes of appropriate male and female behavior: we have defined fantasy as the exploration of new worlds distant from the home, but it is with home and family that girls are expected to be concerned. If we note Cramer and Hogan's (1975) finding that boys and girls express what they consider "exciting fantasies" in different ways, we must recognize that the definitions used in the present study do not reflect this.

Pitcher and Prelinger (1963) and later Ames (1966) were also concerned with the amount of fantasy in the stories they studied, though both operationalized their concern somewhat differently. They reached the same general conclusion that we have done: as age rises, there is a gradual expansion in the scope of the world dealt with in stories, and a gradual shift toward more fantasy in the action as a whole. Both studies also found that boys tend to venture further afield in their stories, and girls to remain closer to home.

The Interaction of Form and Content

The notion that fantasy and poetic form may both be resources at the disposal of the storyteller is worth exploring further. We can ask if the options which children take up as they tell their stories are chosen at random, or if they bear some specifiable relation to the task at hand.

Bullough (1912), in a classic essay, introduced the notion of "psychical distance" to help explain why the formal element in aesthetic experience tends to frame and separate art from other experience. He argued that distancing helps the reader and the artist reduce the threat posed by the material with which they are dealing. Holland (1968) has elaborated this notion, pointing out that there are really two dimensions involved in the notion of distancing: on the one hand we separate the work of art from our practical, immediate lives. On the other, and partly by virtue of that separation, we allow ourselves to become deeply involved in the aesthetic experience because we know we will not have to act on it.

The notion that certain formal devices can be used to allow greater involvement in threatening situations by removing stories from the main business of life is the one in which we are most interested here. We will be asking whether it is possible to relate the conventions we have studied (openings, closings, past tense), the use of fantasy, and the inclusion of the narrator to the themes and problems that appear in stories children tell.[2]

Defining the Degree of Threat

Defining the degree of threat in stories such as these is itself difficult. We know nothing about the individual children, and nothing relevant about the context in which the stories were told. We can, however, judge the actions against a general background of "social acceptability."[3] Such a classification assumes a cultural norm or standard; it sets up a criterion of the "Is it proper for X to do that" variety, rather than asking, "Was Y, in telling a story about X doing that, dealing with a problem that was personally significant?"

The actions in the stories in the Pitcher and Prelinger (1963) collection range from the socially taboo to the perfectly conventional. Olive's story, in which "him banged the daddy," falls at one extreme, Tess's at the other:

> A little fishie what got killed. His daddy came running. His daddy spanked him. He was crying. Then he went in the bed. Then him banged the daddy. Then she said, "Get out you Daddy," because he spanked the little baby. He was so sad. Then he got some soda out of the kitchen. Then he drinked it all up.
>
> —Olive B., 3 yr 2 mo (P. 66)

> She has her lunch and her daddy's gonna teach her how to swim and they ate on the beach. A picnic because it wasn't in the house. They ate sandwiches, hamburger, and drank each day outside, because they were going swimming each day and they didn't want to waste any time. They didn't eat, because they were getting kind of fat, and they wanted to get thin again.
>
> —Tess B., 4 yr 2 mo (P. 110)

Notice in Tess's story that a narrative in which the action is socially acceptable is not necessarily a "dry run"; it is, however, less disturbing, closer to the mode of friendly, quiet conversation than to that of defending or challenging a view of the world. In addition to the stories that deal with clearly acceptable or clearly taboo activities, there are some intermediate kinds in which characters are hurt or sick through no fault of their own, or in which violence and disorder occur within a context in which they are conventionally accepted—such things as shooting bad guys, hunting, fighting among cowboys and Indians, and so on. Barry's pirates illustrate the type quite well:

> Once there was a boat; pirates were on it. There was a boat with bad pirates on it. Then they had an old cannon and they shot the boat with a bullet and the boat sank. Then the pirates went to sleep in their house.
>
> —Barry M., 3 yr 11 mo (P. 40)

The status of such a story is somewhat ambiguous; the actions are of types which would ordinarily be proscribed, but which are

sanctioned by convention within these "adventure" contexts.[4]
We will return to the problem of how to interpret them after
presenting some of the results.

Distancing and the Acceptability of the Action

Viewing the stories in this way, we do find some evidence of
distancing in the stories in the Pitcher and Prelinger (1963)
collection. Three techniques in particular seem responsive to the
type of actions depicted: the use of realistic characters, the use
of a consistent past tense, and the inclusion of the narrator in
the action of the story. (Changes in the amount of fantasy in the
action were not examined, since this measure is thoroughly confounded with the measure of "acceptability.") Of the two- and
three-year-olds who tell stories with socially acceptable actions,
for example, 94 percent use a realistic setting, 39 percent include themselves in the narrative, and 56 percent tell the story
partly in the present tense. (Dialogue was excluded in calculat-
ing this measure.) Of those who tell stories with unacceptable
actions, on the other hand, only 69 percent use realistic settings,
13 percent include themselves in the narrative, and 19 percent
tell the story partly in the present tense. Four- and five-year-olds
show a similar pattern in their choice of setting, but do not
make similar use of the other options—their stories are so consistently set in the past, and so consistently about characters
other than themselves, that there is little room left to further
distance threatening stories in these ways.

Neither the use of formal openings nor the use of formal
closings shows any relationship to the acceptability of the actions
in these stories. Apparently these reflect expectations about
what a story—any story—is like, and are not varied in response
to these sorts of demands.[5]

These results can be related to our model of language use as
it was presented in chapter 2. Pitcher and Prelinger (1963) assert
that there are certain phase-specific themes that emerge from
the psychoanalytic literature in general and from this particular collection of stories in particular—themes which represent especially important developmental issues, focal points of

concern during the years before six. In a high proportion of instances, stories which attempt to come to terms with one or another of these developmental problems are also stories which involve actions which violate acceptable social conventions: someone hits a parent, forgets their toilet training, or is abandoned unloved by someone that had been trusted. In our model of language use, such stories have moved out of the expressive toward articulation or reformulation of the accepted system of values.

A second large group of stories originates much closer to the everyday, accepted world; rather than exploring developmental themes, they relax within the comfortable confines of a world which is posing no immediate problem. If the developmental themes are relevant to them at all, they are relevant only in the sense that the child has already found a way to handle them, and their content does not intrude to disturb the calm of the story world. This story world is one that works the way the children's expectations have led them to believe it should work, and such expectations are simply used without the need for special affirmation or an attempted reformulation. These are stories in which the actions of the characters are well within the confines of social acceptability, but they are not "empty forms"—any more than the diaries of Boswell or Pepys are empty. But, like those diaries, neither are they responding to strong pressures from either pole of the elaborative choice.

Finally we are left with the adventure stories. Though such stories are often strongly distanced in terms of the measures used here, this distancing can be explained as a purely conventional one, a product of expectations about "adventure stories" rather than of any individual "use" of these resources toward other ends. The worlds of cops and robbers, cowboys and Indians, pirates, and war are worlds that exist for the child only in stories; but they are worlds with which the child of five is very familiar. In a sense, to distance stories by placing them in these worlds is simply to put these characters and actions in the only contexts the child has ever seen them. Rather than accepting such stories as expressions of unconscious wishes and desires, it seems more likely that they are simply explorations of this special story world itself. Many may not even have that much content; they may simply be artifacts of the task situation, garbled repetitions of recent television programs used to meet the investigator's demand, "Tell me a story."

Other Evidence

For the present this is conjectural. With stories taken in isolation as these must be, there is no independent way to assess the degree of involvement and coming to terms which they represent. For the present the evidence is strongly suggestive, if far from conclusive, and the results at least congruent with those of other studies. Ames (1966), for example, tabulated a number of situations which she felt represented ways in which children protect themselves while telling stories. Though age trends were erratic, she concluded that the youngest children had things happen to brothers and sisters, to someone of the opposite sex, to animals, or to objects. Reversal of ill-fortune became important at three; punishment of villainy and toying with the notion of violence without actually allowing it to occur were important in the stories of four- and five-year-olds. Many of these situations, of course, are just the sort of incidents from which the child might want to be detached. To be punished for villainy, for example, leaves open the possibility that it is the child who is the villain.

An experimental study by Boyd and Mandler (1955) takes us further. They were working with older children than we have been considering; the sample included ninety-six third-grade American children with an average age of eight years five months and an average IQ of 101. Boyd and Mandler used four stories with human characters and four with animals; each of these sets included two stories with "good" (socially approved) and two with "bad" (socially disapproved) behavior. Each child heard two stories, and after each story was shown a picture (either of animal or human characters, as another variable in the experimental design) and asked to write a story about it. The resulting stories were analyzed for several aspects of form and content, with several results of direct interest to us. "I" appeared more frequently in response to good content ($p < .07$), punishment in response to bad ($p < .05$). This latter, though not directly related to distancing in our analysis, does support the world-ordering nature of stories: the balance of expectation has been upset by the stimulus and is being restored to some extent in the response.

These were the only significant differences due to the content of the stories. There were differences on all measures except one, however, between human and animal stories. In general, the data suggest more involvement with stories about humans, with concomitant anxiety about any socially disapproved behavior. The effect of substituting animal for human characters at this age seems to be to remove the stories to a realm in which the implications will be less threatening. Supporting this is the additional finding that 74 percent of the children preferred animal stories, a natural result if animal stories are in general less anxiety-provoking. Whether results would be the same with younger children, who tend to blend animal and human characters with little distinction in their stories, is less certain.

Problem Solving

Distancing is also related to the general problem of the complexity of stories. If a story is interpreted through the reader's or listener's system of constructs, then the events in the story will tend to validate or invalidate that system. The more central the constructs are to the person's representation of the world, the more complex and far-reaching will be the effects of any difficulty the story creates. To change central constructs, those which structure expectations about the taken for granted world of immediate experience, may involve so many realignments that the problem may simply become too complex, too threatening, to handle. Distancing in the terms we have been discussing it is one way in which this complexity can be reduced to a manageable level. Even as it increases the total conceptual complexity by extending the world beyond the immediate confines of home and family, it also provides a "scene" of action whose implications will be less directly related to a person's central constructs and which will, as one result, be less complex to order and understand. By being involved less directly in the story, a person may be able to find solutions to predicaments which otherwise might not even be acknowledged.

Many of the stories depicting "unacceptable" actions are striking illustrations of this. Children use them to discover for themselves some of the consequences of such actions as killing their parents—actions which, we must suppose, they never have attempted and never will attempt "in real" instead of "in story." These explorations do not have to be interpreted as expressions of unconscious conflicts or wish fulfillment (though in a few cases they may be); it is more to our present point to recognize that these actions derive directly from the conventional set of social expectations. To set a norm is to create the possibility of violating that norm; to understand the norm means learning what counts as violating as well as what counts as observing it. By removing the characters and setting from their own immediate sphere of experience, children are given a simple way to explore these norms without threatening other important constructs. They can see what happens to "bad people" without doing anything which would conflict with their expectations about what they, as "good people," do. Or as Bettelheim (1976) describes it in discussing a more particular example, "The fantasy of the wicked stepmother not only preserves the good mother intact, it also prevents having to feel guilty about one's angry thoughts and wishes about her—a guilt which would seriously interfere with the good relation to Mother" (p. 69). Bettelheim goes on to suggest that a child's fantasies are also an important means of understanding, of figuring out "what the specific consequences of some action might be.... It is his way of 'playing with ideas'" (p. 119).

We can see such processes at work in the examples provided by Griffiths (1935), who obtained a wide variety of fantasy products from a relatively small sample of five-year-olds. Alfred told her one such series of stories, spread over nine school days. The first two stories, told two days apart, set out the experience he is in the process of assimilating:

> Once upon a time there was a boy, and he went out fishing, and he saw a fish in the water, a ... a ... a big one. So he

got his net out, but he didn't want that big fish, he wanted only his little fish.

> Once upon a time there was a boy and he went out fishing, and he saw a big fish in the water, and this big fish popped up and ate the boy all up.

As Griffiths puts it, he has yet to resolve "how to avoid being devoured by the fishes when one goes fishing." During the succeeding interviews, Alfred's stories explore a variety of approaches to this basic issue: in the third, the fish simply catch themselves, even walking across a bit of land to climb into the collecting jar. In the fourth he simply avoids the topic, sending his character off to the country; there he picked some buttercups and "he didn't do nothing else." By the fifth in the series, he is back to the water's edge, dipping his net, but the fish still climb in of their own volition. Next he loses his fishing gear, "so he didn't have no jar to put his fishes in." By the seventh interview in this series, Alfred has begun to master the problem, turning it into a joke and laughing heartily:

> Once, er, once upon a time, wait a minute I just thinking . . . a boy went out, he went fishing, and a lil fish jumped on his nose.

This humorous inversion—strongly reminiscent of the reality confirmation through nonsense discussed in chapter 3—seems to have been a final step in construing this experience, leaving Alfred's world once more at ease with the problem of fishing:

> Once upon a time, a boy went out fishing, and he brought a *big* fish home in his jar, and a lot of little ones. (Pp. 180–81)

Summary

Data presented in this chapter provide less satisfactory evidence about the issues under discussion than we have been able to muster in earlier chapters. To an uncomfortable extent, the effects of most interest are confounded with one another and the results capable of more than one interpretation. Still some of the findings are clear, and the others are suggestive.

The data demonstrate that as children mature, they are able to explore in their stories patterns of behavior which are further and further removed from their immediate experience. The two-year-olds studied set 97 percent of their stories in the immediate world of home and family; within that setting, the majority of the actions depicted are ones with which they are also familiar (eating, sleeping, crying, spanking). By five, only one-third of the stories remained situated in or near the home, and only 7 percent involved fully realistic actions and behavior. If the results are conceptualized in terms of Bullough's (1912) "psychical distancing," the stories of the five-year-olds are much more fully distanced than those of their younger peers.

The gradual development of new resources both of form and fantasy provide the child with an expanding range of options which can be systematically exploited in organizing and assimilating the patterned experience which a story offers. In particular, both the older and the younger children studied sought to remove from the sphere of immediate experience stories whose content posed any sort of threat; the younger children especially tended to distance these in both setting and time, as well as to leave the narrator out of the narrative. But the fact that the measures of threat and of distancing were both derived from the same source material makes this a finding very much in need of experimental confirmation.

Six

The Response of the Child

Introduction

So far, we have concentrated on children's expectations about the spectator role as reflected in the stories they tell. Telling stories is, of course, only one aspect of spectator-role experience, and for most of us, most of the time, it is probably not even the most important part. Much of our life is spent listening to or reading stories told by others, whether these are simply anecdotes inserted into a conversation, television dramas, or extensive "works of literature" around which large bodies of scholarship and criticism may have accumulated. The process of response is equally as interesting as that of production; indeed any firm line between the two will inevitably blur as we pursue their implications.

Response to the spectator role can take many different forms, only a few of which are verbal (see Cappa 1958; Jones and Buttrey 1970). Nonetheless most studies of response have concentrated on the verbal, both because these are very typical and characteristic responses, and because the methodological problems are less intractable. We will be continuing in this tradition here, though occasional links with nonverbal behavior will suggest themselves.

Verbal responses to spectator-role experience usually take the form of transactional discussions of spectator-role writing. Such discussions reflect many aspects of children's developing thought: their expectations about the spectator role, knowledge of the social conventions which structure life as well as literature, and of course the broad patterns of intellectual organization which structure their thinking. Piaget's theories of intellectual development provide the most thoroughly developed framework for analyzing changes in the nature of the rules underlying thought processes. His studies have been wide-ranging, and though he has not specifically studied literary or artistic response, his findings are highly relevant in these areas as well.

Objective and Subjective Modes

Before we can apply a Piagetian mode of analysis to children's responses to stories, however, we need to recall Susanne Langer's (1967) distinction between objective and subjective modes of feeling. In chapter 2, we saw that subjective feeling arises within us, as the result of internal activities, while objective feeling has its source outside of us. Literary response inevitably involves both: on the one hand there is the "verbal artifact" itself, an objective construct in words and sounds, and on the other there is the pattern of subjective feeling prompted by that construct and controlled through poetic techniques.[1] When we write or talk about our objective response to a story, we are concerned with its publicly verifiable characteristics; these range from precise details of character or setting to consideration of theme or structure or point of view. Though the complexity of a work of literature may lead us to disagree about these characteristics, especially at the more complex levels of analysis, such disagreements are ultimately disagreements about the application of shared conventions of communication.

When we describe our subjective, personal response, on the other hand, we are describing the product of the interaction of the work with our own particular representation of experience. The feeling that results is the product of an internal, personal, slow process of assimilation and accommodation, a process which cannot in principle be described by reference to publicly verifiable conventions. (We can agree on the characteristics of an adventure story, for example, but we will not be able to agree on which adventure story each of us will find most exciting.) This personal response also begins with the stimulus provided by the work and with our conventions for interpreting it, but it varies with our total state of mind at the time of contact—how tired we are feeling, what distractions there are, what problems are bothering us most. Just as the child's knowledge of the rules and conventions relevant to the objective characteristics of a work shows developmental changes, so do his or her perceptions of the subjective response. We will find that attempts to express (in transactional language) these two aspects of response show characteristic—and separable—patterns of development.

The Nature of Evaluation

In taking up Langer's distinction between objective and subjective in this context, we need to be careful not to reduce it
simply to a distinction between responses which "evaluate" and
those which "describe." By "objective response" we mean the
recognition of some characteristic which seems to lie directly
in the work: that it has 250 pages, two main characters, a
comic subplot, and so on. By "subjective response" we mean
the recognition of the effect of the work on the reader or
listener: that it was thought-provoking or pleasant or too dull
to finish. Both objective and subjective responses are in one
sense "descriptive": the first describes the story; the second, our
personal reaction to it. Rather than paralleling these two types
of response, evaluation seems to be a superordinate process
which subsumes both.[2] Not only are most things evaluated, but
the way in which they are evaluated becomes a more or less
permanent part of our memory of the response (see Cermak
et al. 1972).

Lines of Evidence

In considering the developmental course of the way children
formulate their response to the spectator role, we will be drawing on a number of converging lines of evidence. In one phase of
the present study, samples of children at six, nine, thirteen, and
seventeen were asked to discuss a story of their own choice. Six-
and nine-year-olds were asked, "What is your favorite story?
Tell me about it." Older children received a questionnaire,
part of which asked, "Pick any story or poem you know well and
write about it."[3]

Since the wording of this question seemed likely to bias responses toward retelling the story, two further discussion tasks
were included. The first asked six- and nine-year-olds in a
separate sample, "What is the story of *Little Red Riding Hood*
about?" The second followed a reading of the poem "The Blind
Men and the Elephant" with "What do you think of that

story?" and later, "What was the story I just read you about?"

Another line of evidence, drawn from the same children who were asked to discuss their favorite stories, focused on the explanations which children would offer when pushed for reasons for liking or not liking particular stories. Finally, to examine the way in which children assign meaning to spectator-role writing, all of the children studied were asked about the meaning of selected common sayings.

As we will see in this chapter, the results from each of these lines of inquiry reinforce and support the results from the others; response processes seem consistent across the various tasks, and also consistent with the findings of other investigators. These findings, which will be drawn on in a general way in the present chapter and returned to more fully at the end of chapter 7, have been summarized by Squire (1969), Purves and Beach (1972), D'Arcy (1973), and Applebee (1977).

Allowing children to nominate their own stories for discussion differs considerably from the approach taken in most other investigations. As Kelly (1955) has argued in discussing his own diagnostic and clinical procedures, allowing a child to nominate examples of the domain under investigation is an effective means to insure that all children are faced with a comparable task. The alternative of asking for reactions to a particular story brings in a range of variables which are difficult to control— differences in reading or listening ability, previous experience with similar stories, even the amount of time various children need to spend in assimilating the experience will all contribute to differences in the initial expressed response. By asking for discussions of stories already known and similarly evaluated (as "favorites"), this initial process of assimilation is bypassed in order to look more directly at the meaning stories are given by the child, rather than at the process of giving that meaning in the first place.[4] This is an especially important distinction to make in the study of response to literature, for which there is good evidence that the giving of meaning is a slow, contemplative process involving significant changes over relatively long periods of time (Britton 1954; Wilson 1966; Harding 1968). The use of *Little Red Riding Hood* lies somewhat closer to previous investigations, in that all children were asked to respond to the same story; it was a story chosen, however, as one which each would already know.

In considering children's verbal descriptions of stories, we will find major changes corresponding at least roughly to the changes Piaget has delineated in other domains of thinking. For the remainder of this chapter, we will explore the development of children's ability to discuss (and represent to themselves and others) the world of a story as they progress from preoperational to concrete operational modes of thought. In the following chapter, we will turn to the advent of formal operations and the new possibilities of response which they bring.

Discussing the Action

When six- and nine-year-old children are asked to discuss a story at some length, the mode of response which requires the least reorganization of material is simply to retell the story, complete with title, formal opening and closing lines, and dialogue. This is in fact the most common mode of "telling about" favorite stories for the six-year-old children studied: 50 percent used it, and another 27 percent refused to answer because they were worried that they might not remember it well enough (table 3). Responses by children who were asked what *Little Red Riding Hood* is "about" show a similar pattern, in spite of a greater tendency for this question to produce lists of characters (recorded as "Summary" in table 3).

Eric's contribution is a good example of the retellings, and illustrates both the length and the detail which is often involved.

Once there was the three little pigs. And they asked the man with some straws, "Can we have some straws?" says the first little pig. And he gave them some straws and he built a straw house. In came the wol-, the wolf. He puffed and he puffed and he blew the house down. And he puffed and he puffed. And when the house fell down and so three little, the second three little pig went to the man with some sticks and he said to the man, "Can I have some sticks for to build a house?" And then the man said, "Yes," says the man and he gave him some sticks. And when he built the house up and he was, and he puffed and he puffed, and he puffed and he puffed. And he blew all the sticks all fell down. And then he went to the man with some bricks. He said, "Can I have some bricks for the house, to build a house?" "Yes," said the man, and he gave him some bricks.

So when he built the house of bricks, the wolf came along and blew the house down but he couldn't. So one day the wolf came and said to the, to the second pig, "Shall we go to Farmer Field's house, Farmer Field's grass?" And he said, "Alright." And then he did go already but the wolf came back and he said, "Let's go to it now." And he said, "I've been to the Farm Field's house." So he said, "Let's go and go to the next field and pick some apples, there's an apple tree there. So we can pick some." So first he went to the apple tree and picked some apples. And then it was so fat and so he runned away and the apple went down the hill into the road. So the three little, the pig went into the, into the churn and he went around and he runned the wolf over. And he said, "I runned you over." Then he rolled back to the house. And then ... so ... then the wolf went in the chimney pot and the three little pig put some water, some hot water in then and then he fell down into the pot, "Plop." And he lived happily ever after.

—Eric M., 6 yr 1 mo

Eric is by no means alone in the detail he uses; his is not even the longest of the retellings which the six-year-olds produced. (For further details about the length and complexity of response at each age, see appendix 2 and supplementary table 12, appendix 3.)

Such narrative is very typical of the type of response that would be expected during Piaget's preoperational period. During this stage, representation is highly concrete, taking the form of "an isomorphic step-by-step mental replica of concrete actions and events" (Flavell 1963, p. 158). There is little or no reorganization of events into superordinate categories or more general schematizations; the child has great difficulty in integrating individual elements from the story into any sort of general framework. Concrete operational thought, on the other hand, brings with it a new ability to classify and organize: instead of a set of elements enactively chained together, symbolic representations involve a reorganization of experience into hierarchies of categories and subcategories, with specifiable relationships between them.

This ability to classify leads to responses which are best described as *summaries* of the events in a story: rather than retelling the story, the summary tells "what it is about." Richard and Barbara both gave such summary responses in writing about particular stories:

> I think that the Famous Five stori's are quite good. In the storis there is a lot of adventure and a lot of things happen. They get bad luke at the beginning and thing all kam out all right in the end.
>
> —Richard O., 9 yr 3 mo
>
> Cinderella is a grile that had very nies invengeras [adventures].
>
> —Barbara T., 9 yr 1 mo

The summaries of six- and nine-year-olds are typically very short, and make little or no use of the formal markers of the story mode that appear so prominently in their retellings. Instead, these discussions usually subsume the events of the story within a more general category—"adventure," "lovely end," "nice," and so on. The simple "The story is . . ." sentence structure is often used, which leads in turn to a relatively simple syntactic structure, with correspondingly short T-units (see supplementary table 10, appendix 3).[5]

The other type of response which was scored as summarization in the present study was the character list that occurred in telling what *Little Red Riding Hood* was about. Whether this is summary in the same sense is problematic; it can be interpreted as the result of a syncretistic focus on isolated features, rather than as the result of powers of categorization. If character lists are removed from the data in table 3, 4.5 percent of the remaining six-year-olds and 27.3 percent of the nine-year-olds respond with summarization of *Little Red Riding Hood*—remarkably close to the results for favorite stories.

In discussing the content of stories, some children resorted to an expanded form of summary, as Barbara did in discussing *Sleeping Beauty:*

> It's about a man and a lady that . . . . The lady falls asleep cause she hurt her hand on the spinning wheel. And she fell

asleep. And the witch that made her to do it said she, that she'll sleep for a hundred years. Then after the hundred years the prince came and kissed her and they all woke up in the palace. And everyone woke up and it was, and then they got married and it was very nice. It was a lovely end and everything.

—Barbara T., 9 yr 1 mo

This seems to fall onto a continuum between complete retelling and complete summarization; much of it is synopsis or paraphrase. Whereas retellings frankly attempt to retell the story in its original form and summaries attempt to encapsulate the plot within a more general category, the synopsis is almost a report of ongoing events. Usually this results in some condensation, but the synopsis can be as long as the storytelling itself. Rebecca's account of *Little Red Riding Hood* is another good example:

Well, it's about a little girl and her nannie makes her, makes her a red cloak. And, a, one day her nannie's not well and her mother sends her out with something to give to her nannie and she meets a big bad wolf and the big bad wolf asks her where she's going and she tells him. She rushes off to there and a, the grandmother's not there so he get dressed up in grandmother's nighties and gets into bed. Red Riding comes along, knocks on the door, and he tells her to come in. And she goes in, and, a, she gives him some things and she says, "Oh grandmother what big teeth you got, what big ears and what big eyes you got." And when she says teeth goes the better to eat you with and he jumps out of bed and runs after her. And the huntsman, a, gets him and chop his head off. Now Little Red Riding Hood can go and see her grandmother as often as she likes.

—Rebecca C., 10 yr 1 mo

A synopsis usually starts with "It is about . . . ," continues in the present tense, and reports rather than recreates the dialogue. Rebecca, for example, does not change her tone of voice in reciting the dialogue in her discussion, though she repeats much of it word for word. Many children simply condense what is said: "She says, 'What big eyes you got' and all that" (Nicholas H., 4 yr 8 mo).[6]

Table 3   Children's Mode of Discussing Stories

	Children (%)			
	Favorite		*Red Riding Hood*	
Mode	Age 6 (n=22)	Age 9 (n=22)	Age 6 (n=22)	Age 9 (n=22)
No response	27.3	0.0	9.1	0.0
Retelling	50.0	9.1	31.8	4.5
Any synopsis	13.6	40.9	13.6	36.4
Any summary	4.5	31.8	45.5	59.1
Evaluation only	4.5	18.2	0.0	0.0
Chi-square (age)[a]	10.83***		4.48*	

[a] Comparing retellings with synopsis and summary combined, $df=1$. On tests of significance, see appendix 1.

* $p < .05$, two-tailed.

*** $p < .005$, two-tailed.

Synopsis seems to be a transitional form which comes between the enactive retelling of the young child and the classificatory summary of the slightly older one. Certainly it is relatively rare among the six-year-olds studied, though by nine it accounts for 41 percent of the responses to a favorite story and 36 percent of those to *Little Red Riding Hood*. Summary also begins to be prominent at nine in response to both stories.[7]

Discussions of the Fable

The differences between discussions of favorite stories and those of *Little Red Riding Hood*—particularly the character lists which the latter provoked—emphasize the importance of the particular question chosen in soliciting responses from young children. Their responses indicate that when children think they are being asked to talk at some length, the response of six-year-olds, at least, is to attempt to retell it. Responses to John

Godfrey Saxe's version of "The Blind Men and the Elephant"[8] shed some light on what happens when the wording of the question creates a different expectation. This is a rhymed fable in eight stanzas (a ninth stanza drawing an explicit moral was omitted), the middle six of which describe the reactions of six blind men to their encounters with an elephant. The first blind man, for example, stumbles against the elephant's side and declares, "God bless me, but the elephant is very like a wall." In this version the poem is quite difficult for children even at nine, especially as administered with a single reading and no accompanying pictures or explanation. The language is bizarre and there is no real plot or narrative structure to lead the child from one incident to the next.

After listening to a reading of the poem, each child was asked, "What do you think of that story?" and then, "What was the story I just read you about?"

The two questions produced very different sorts of responses. At both six and nine, "What do you think of that story?" produced a short, universally positive reaction from all but a handful of the forty-four children (for example, "It's nice" or "I liked it"). Nine of the six-year-olds and three of the nine-year-olds did not answer the question; one six-year-old responded instead, "It's hard." The second question, "What is the story about?" led to a (not always accurate) focus on the characters:

It's about six men and a elephant who was blind.
—Clifford C., 5 yr 10 mo

It's about six blind men and elephants.
—Marissa C., 9 yr 6 mo

Responses to this question did suggest a difference in the way some of the six- and nine-year-olds approached the task. At nine, 31.8 percent of the children amplified their character list with some sort of summary of the situation in which the characters were involved:

It's about six blind men who go to see an elephant.
—Lloyd J., 9 yr 11 mo

It's about these men from Indostan. They came to see the elephant but they were all blind. [Continues with an attempt to retell the fable.]

—Doreen B., 10 yr 0 mo

Only one of the six-year-olds made this sort of elaboration.

Other questions that were asked about the fable sampled the child's comprehension and ability to retell it. As one would expect, older children were consistently better at such tasks. A measure of the number of accurate details included in their retellings is indicative of performance on various measures: six-year-olds averaged 6.7 correct details, nine-year-olds averaged 15.9.[9]

The National Assessment of Educational Progress (1973b) also looked at oral responses of nine-year-olds to a short story and two poems. Responses were scored to indicate whether they had at least one statement that could be classified as engagement-involvement, perception, interpretation, evaluation, or retelling. As in the reaction to the fable in the present study, the nine-year-olds in the National Assessment sample tended to respond initially with a positive evaluation ("It's pretty good"); as a result an average of 58 percent of the responses included some evaluation and 65 percent included some expression of engagement-involvement. There was also a strong tendency, in addition to this global reaction, to focus on the action of the story or poem: an average of 43 percent involved some of what the National Assessment called retelling (a category that did not separate out summary, synopsis, and narrative responses as we have done). Responses that could be called interpretation or perception occurred much less frequently.[10]

Evaluation

A short, positive evaluation was children's major type of response when asked what they "thought about" "The Blind Men and the Elephant," and was also a major response type in the National Assessment samples. To examine the extent to which children are able to defend such evaluations, the forty-four children who had separately discussed their favorite stories were asked *why* they liked or disliked specific stories which they had earlier evaluated. Their responses make clear both the extent to which evaluations are integrated into a fuller representation of the story, and the extent to which children have begun to recognize and separate their own objective and subjective reactions.

Early Forms

Piaget has described many characteristics of preoperational thinking which are the result of the very simple forms of representation used by the child. One feature is *egocentrism*; there is little awareness of the demands of communication and little orientation toward the needs of the listener. As a result, there is little compunction to justify a chain of reasoning, nor is there much awareness of contradictory or paradoxical conclusions. Another feature of the reasoning of the preoperational child is a tendency to focus attention on a single, striking detail of an experience, to the neglect of other important aspects. Piaget has called this phenomenon *centration*.

The preoperational stage in the evaluation of stories shows several parallels with these characteristics of preoperational thinking in other domains. When asked to explain why they like stories, children will say "It's nice" or "It's good," and pushed about why it is nice, will respond with a circular "Because I like it." When elaboration occurs, it is usually linked syncretistically to one or another memorable incident in the story, rather than integrated into a conceptualization of the whole. There are many examples of such centration from children in the present study:

> You said you liked the story 'Hanzel and Gretel'. Why did you like it?—*They got the money and the gold.*—You said you did not like the story 'Little Red Riding Hood'. Why didn't you like it?—*He eats the grandma.*
> —Jon M., 6 yr 2 mo

> You said you liked the story 'Cinderella'. Why?—*It's nice.*— Why do you think it is a nice story?—*She went to the ball.*— You said you did not like the story about the three little pigs. Why not?—*They get all eaten up.*
> —Joe P., 5 yr 10 mo

I like *The Lion, the Witch, and the Wardrobe* because when the children were playing Hide-in-seek one hid in the wardrobe and hid behind the clothes and found herself in a cold snowy land.

—Helen A., 10 yr 1 mo

Such answers often seem quite appropriate, since the most vivid incidents in a story are often central to the overall development of the plot; but whereas the adult may cite the incident as an exemplification of the story as a whole, the young child's response does not have this broader structure to guide it. Many of the details seized upon are thus irrelevant from the adult's point of view—as when *Peter Rabbit* is deemed a sad story because poor Mr. McGregor has no lettuce left to eat.

It is this lack of an integrative superstructure which is the most characteristic feature of responses at this stage. Both the global "I like it because it is good" and the syncretistic focus on specific incidents reflect the lack of a framework for integrating the evaluation into the rest of the child's memory or experience of the story. Such unintegrated responses were given by 68.2 percent of the twenty-two six-year-olds, dropping to 27.3 percent of the twenty-two nine-year-olds. More specifically, centration on a specific incident occurred at least once in 36.4 percent of the responses at six, 18.2 percent at nine, while the circular "I like it because it is good" was given by 50 percent at six, falling to 13.6 percent at nine.[11]

Evaluation as a Class Attribute

Piaget's descriptions of concrete operational thinking emphasize the extent to which it is concerned with class membership, and beyond this, with classes organized into hierarchic systems. In place of the enactive, nonreversible relationships of the preoperational child, at the concrete operational stage the child becomes able to move up and down class hierarchies, interpreting new experiences in terms of preexisting categories, and setting the categories themselves into various relationships with other systems of classification. Categorizations based on one set of experiences become available for classification of other experiences, and such class operations as addition, subtraction, and identity become available to the child.

Thus it is at the concrete operational stage that evaluation first becomes systematic. As children become aware of their responses to a story, they begin to classify them into categories with clearly marked attributes. It is these categories which seem to be evaluated, rather than the specific details of the story itself. When they describe their subjective response, we find children claiming that a book is "interesting," "dreary," or "just plain funny." Such characteristics seem to be attributed directly to the book, though in fact they are descriptions of the way the book has affected the particular reader. The evaluation of a story is often closely associated with this description of the subjective response, but it is not identical with it. Children do not find it repetitive to say, for example, "Sometimes stories are dull and I don't like them" (Laura B., 9 yr 11 mo).

Objective responses are similarly treated as belonging to classes with relatively clear-cut attributes. The selection of attributes sometimes seems "analytic," focusing on parts of a work such as its "rhyme" or "rhythm," but these are used to define a class (of "works that have rhyme" or "works that have rhythm") rather than as a means of exploring the structure of a particular work. Other attributes which children select tend to be situational; content is treated literally rather than as embodying a point or message of a wider generality. Stories are enjoyed because they are about "cowboys" or "families" or "trains," not because they are about "how families work" or "problems of good and evil."

At this level there is little spontaneous attempt to relate objective and subjective responses to one another, though some children notice that they occur together. Helen's answer is typical:

I do not like *Heartsease* because it is hard to understand and is also boring.

—Helen A., 10 yr 1 mo

Other children note in the same breath that they like adventure stories *and* they like exciting stories.

At nine, 90.1 percent of the children studied made use of some categorization in giving reasons for their evaluations of stories, a statistically significant ($p < .05$) increase over the 50.0 percent found at age six.

Literalism

In both the preoperational and concrete operational periods, symbolic representations are tied quite directly to the concrete world of the child's experience. There is little generalization beyond this experience, and little awareness of alternative views. This produces a literalism which has been apparent in the focus on the action of the story, as well as in the simple categorizations which have been used for subjective, personal responses. It is legitimate to ask, however, whether children may also recognize a more generalized meaning, even if they do not ordinarily think it necessary to verbalize it.

We can explore the extent to which the findings so far parallel the ability of the young child to draw meaning from a story by looking at children's explanations of common sayings. Kenneth Burke (1957, pp. 253 ff.) has treated proverbs as the prototypical literary form; without making that strong a claim, we are assuming here that the way in which common sayings are interpreted will be directly related to the way in which more complex spectator-role experiences are interpreted. Each of the forty-four six- and forty-four nine-year-olds interviewed was asked to explain either "You must have gotten out of the wrong side of the bed this morning," or "When the cat is away, the mice will play." In general, children before the age of eleven or twelve are not successful in specifying adult meanings for such sayings (Piaget 1926; Watts 1944), but they are very consistent in their own attempts to make sense of them. Almost universally, their interpretation is a literal one. Thus at six:

> "You must have gotten out of the wrong side of the bed this morning."
> *But I don't! I go around to the right side.*
> —Eric M., 6 yr 1 mo
> *No, I haven't.*—What would it mean if someone said it to you though?—*They'd be telling me wrong.*
> —Sam C., 5 yr 9 mo

"When the cat is away, the mice will play."
The cat is shopping, and the cat likes the mouse.—Could it mean anything about children?—*The children have a cat and a mouse.*

—Colin C., 5 yr 11 mo

That means the mice will play all over the room and look for cheese. And when the cat comes back he'll hurry right in his hole.—Could it mean anything about children?—*One child's got a cat and one child's got a mouse.*

—Terrence P., 5 yr 10 mo

Such literal interpretations were offered by 50 percent of the twenty-two six-year-olds asked about the wrong side of the bed, and by 86 percent of those asked about the cat and mouse. In both cases, none of the remaining children claimed to understand the saying at all.[12]

By nine, children in these samples began to show some understanding of the wrong side of the bed. Their answers varied, but most were related to the situation of having slept poorly:

You're not awake yet.

—Robert W., 9 yr 2 mo

Dosy.

—Frank M., 10 yr 1 mo

You're grumpy.

—Helen A., 10 yr 1 mo

Only a few children had begun to move beyond the literal level in explaining the other saying, however:

It means if somebody is away, the other person will do something they're not supposed to.—Does it mean anything about cats and mice?—*Not really.*

—Doreen B., 10 yr 0 mo

Cause when the cat is away, when the cat is here the mice don't come out cause they know the cat would eat them but when the cat is away they always come out and play.—Do you think it might mean something about children?—*Pardon?*—Do you think it might mean something about children?—*Yes. Because sometimes they have fights and if they have a fight they know that somebody wants to do it again they don't want to come out, but if they're away they want to come out.*

—Belgin C., 9 yr 2 mo

Such hints of understanding were rare: only 9 percent of the nine-year-olds gave them without prompting with the question about children, and even with prompting the figure rose only to 27 percent. For the wrong side of the bed, on the other hand, some 64 percent of the nine-year-olds showed some degree of understanding. The difference in the proportion of children moving beyond the literal level in response to the two sayings is highly significant,[13] but the explanation is unclear. It may be that the lack of logic which six-year-olds see in getting out of the wrong side of the bed pushes older children to look beyond the literal answer. Or it may be that the generally accepted meaning is itself situationally derived, based on a loose association between sleeping poorly, "wrong" beds, and poor behavior. This type of reasoning does become accessible during the concrete operational period, and should be available to many of the nine-year-olds in these samples. More evidence is needed, but it is likely that both the inadequacy of the literal interpretation and the availability of the situationally based one contribute to the results.

These findings with common sayings have parallels in studies by Gardner et al. (1975) and Billow (1975) of metaphor comprehension and production. Gardner et al. (1975) constructed a series of metaphor completion tasks, of the form "He looks as gigantic as ——." Children were asked to complete the sentence, as well as to pick the most appropriate ending from a prepared set of literal, conventional, appropriate, and inappropriate endings. In studies of children at selected ages between three and nineteen, they found that the endings chosen by nursery school children showed no clear preference. By age seven, however, 75 percent of the endings selected were literal; by eleven, the preference had shifted to conventional endings (chosen by 71 percent). The choice of "conventional" endings can be interpreted as the result of a concrete operational process of choice from among a set of "proper endings for metaphors." Billow (1975), studying fifty boys between the ages of five and thirteen, found that metaphors based on similarity (for example, "Hair is spaghetti") became accessible with the classificatory skills of concrete operations. He also found that at earlier ages a significant proportion of metaphors can be understood intuitively by the child, without the aid of concrete operational processes. Billow's study is particularly interesting (and unusual) in its careful analysis of the operations involved in metaphors of various type, and of the relationships between these operations and the child's ability to solve similar problems not involving metaphor.

Summary

The evidence presented in this chapter suggests that before adolescence there are at least two distinct stages in the way children represent their spectator-role experiences to themselves and to others; these stages have characteristics which correspond to Piaget's descriptions of preoperational and concrete operational thought in other domains. During the preoperational stage, which lasts until about the age of six or seven, the child's representations seem to take the simplest possible form: a nearly one-to-one correspondence between the representation and the original experience, with little or no evidence of reorganization or recoding. To the extent that the child discusses a story without retelling it during this stage, the discussion reflects such well-known phenomena as centration and egocentrism, with little further sense of structure or logical coherence.

With the advent of concrete operations, the child's responses take on a new organization, one which is apparently based on an ability to organize and classify the experience being confronted. This leads to the first clear verbal separation of objective and subjective responses, though children appear unaware of the distinction between a characteristic of the work and a characteristic of their personal response to it. They do comment on both, however, labeling a story "an adventure" and "exciting" as two separate characteristics. This new ability to categorize also leads to the first relatively extended discussions of stories using transactional techniques; the younger child relies on poetic techniques, reexperiencing the story in the process of retelling it.

Seven

The Response
of the Adolescent

Introduction

The categories and class relationships of concrete operational thought provide preadolescent children with a systematic and powerful method for organizing and understanding their experience. Adolescents, too, make use of such classifications of experience, but for them the classification becomes a subset within a larger classification of all that might occur. It is what Piaget has called "formal operations" that makes this expansion possible. In effect, by observing and organizing the combinations of events around them, adolescents seem to derive rules for combining events which allow them to imagine all of the hypothetically possible combinations of observations, some of which may never occur. Those combinations which emerge as possible but which have never been observed become hypotheses for testing. It is this process of testing which forms the basis of the hypothetical-deductive method of science, allowing for such advances as the systematic untangling of cause and effect— and fundamental advance in the individual's understanding.

This leads to a radical shift in orientation. Instead of being preoccupied with stabilizing their impressions, individuals become concerned with analyzing "how the world works," and in turn considering how it might work differently. This leads to inquiry in virtually all fields of human endeavor—from science on the one hand to politics on the other. In effect, the adolescent replaces the younger child's sense of "what is" with a new sense of "what might be."

Analysis and Generalization

The resources of formal operations have a dramatic effect on the child's response to stories. In place of the preadolescent's concern with summarizing or recreating the action, there is a new concern with analyzing the parts of a story, and with forming generalizations about its meaning.

The characteristic of analysis is that a work is treated in terms of "how it works": its mechanics, the logic of its structure, its images and symbols. Whereas the younger child will order the work into categories based on concrete attributes or characteristics, the adolescent tries to explain the reasons behind those characteristics. The focus shifts to a consideration (implicitly if not explicitly) of how the work *might have been* structured as well as how it *is* structured.[1] Analysis is often integrated with evaluation, as in Jill's discussion:

> I don't know who wrote *Rebecca* but I loved her style of writing. All the time while she was writing she was describing in a different way to others. Always I wanted to see what else would happen—perhaps it was because she used small details. I liked best the bit where she first came to Manderley—I didn't like the mystery bit so much—because it didn't seem so real. I didn't really enjoy the first two chapters. But on the whole I thought it was a good book.
> —Jill V., 13 yr 8 mo

For all her casualness and disorganization, Jill's concern with finding *reasons* for her reactions is evident. As she gains experience in this sort of writing, her responses will take on a more coherent organization, becoming closer in form, perhaps, to Jane's discussion of *The Lord of the Rings:*

> The most important thing about this book, is its almost complete reliance on the imagination of the reader. The actual book has tremendous sustaining power. It is long—comparable in length to 'War and Peace', and yet never becomes boring. This must lie in the authors continual introduction of new elements, and events. The nearest characters to human beings are the people at the inn at the very beginning of the book and Studes. This absence of the human element, gives complete freedom to the imagination.
> The strife between good and evil is tremendous. The book is well written in that the feelings in the "good places" and in bad differ so completely. The central element—the ring is a force that can be felt throughout the book, although is not always specifically stated.
> I find all pictures of the characters in the book, disagreeable, as they seem to ruin the whole effect of the book.
> —Jane E., 17 yr 3 mo

Generalization, on the other hand, while often beginning in analysis, puts its emphasis on the work as the statement of a point of view. The reader may agree with the author or offer an alternative, but the response differs from analysis in that it is now consciously concerned with understanding the world through the work, rather than with understanding the function or structure of the work itself. Again, generalization may be directly linked to evaluation, though it need not be. Roy's discussion of *The Satyricon* takes place almost entirely on this level:

> A book which tells of life before the fall of an empire—the Roman Empire. The book tries to suggest that rather than the fall being attributed to a general loosening in the control exercised over outside powers, it was in fact largely to be blamed upon the corruptions which developed within the Roman Empire. The slackening in control over their own actions, naturally led to the Romans being incapable of preventing the complete collapse of the Empire.
>
> —Roy F., 17 yr 8 mo

Both analysis and generalization require quite a different sort of intellectual process than that involved in the responses of preadolescent children. They require the construction of alternative structures, going beyond the factors presented in the book to others which might have been introduced instead. It is this extrapolation which depends on Piaget's formal operational structures.

These forms of response develop relatively late. When samples of thirty nine-year-old and thirty thirteen-year-old children from a comprehensive high school and its drawing area were asked to discuss a story they knew well, few moved beyond summarization; at thirteen, analysis and generalization together accounted for only 7 percent of the essays. At two highly selective single-sex schools, on the other hand, analysis accounted for over half of the essays at thirteen, though the other 45 percent of the students provided simply a synopsis or plot summary. By seventeen, 60 percent of the pupils analyzed the story in the course of their response, and another 30 percent generalized from it (table 4).[2]

Table 4   Children's Discussions of Stories
                               Known Well

	Comprehensive School (%)		Selective Schools (%)	
	Age 9 (n=30)	Age 13 (n=30)	Age 13 (n=20)	Age 17 (n=20)
1. Retelling	53.3	3.3	. . .	. . .
2. Any synopsis	6.7	30.0	25.0	. . .
3. Any summary	23.3	56.7	20.0	. . .
4. Any analysis	. . .	3.3	55.0	60.0
5. Any generalization	. . .	3.3	. . .	30.0
6. Evaluation only	16.7	3.3	. . .	10.0
	9 vs. 13	13 vs. 13		13 vs. 17
Chi-square tests of age differences	21.83***	14.77***		8.27***
df	2	2		1
Comparing categories[a]	1,2,3	1+2,3,4+5		2+3,4+5

> [a]Categories combined to raise expected
> frequencies to levels appropriate for
> use of chi-square. See appendix 1,
> "Tests of Significance."
> *** $p < .005$.

Evaluation

Analysis

When adolescents are asked to give reasons for liking or not
liking stories, their new powers of analysis produce, on the one
hand, a set of essentially aesthetic criteria, and on the other a
more precise formulation of personal response. Aesthetic criteria for evaluation emerge from adolescents' objective reactions: their assessment of the rhetoric and style of a work, as
well as its overall structure and development. These structural
features are treated as defining the "mechanism" rather than
the category membership of the work. Whereas the younger
child will proclaim, "I don't like it because it rhymes," the older

says, "I don't like it because it rhymes in the wrong places" (Lucy B., 13 yr 5 mo) or "the story is too haphazard" (Sam L., 14 yr 1 mo).

The complexity which adolescents accept in the formal structure of a story is paralleled by a complexity in their personal or subjective response. Instead of summing up a work simply as "exciting" or "dull," adolescents begin to notice changing patterns of response: "the tension rises" or "it lets you down in the end." Sometimes their analyses will lead them to recognize that they empathize with one or another character, or that there are correspondences between their own lives and the situation in the story. This is usually expressed as "identification": "I like to live in them," as Jill V. (13 yr 8 mo) put it; "It makes you feel part of it" (Delilah M., 13 yr 5 mo). Paradoxically, it is precisely when the reader begins to talk of "identification" or "engagement" that the experience becomes further distanced psychologically: the response has become indirect, mediated through the recognition that it is only "*like* I was there," whereas for the younger child it is directly and immediately exciting.

In seeking reasons for their evaluations of stories, it is the thirteen-year-olds studied who first showed a substantial tendency to make use of analysis (table 5). They tended to concentrate on analyzing their objective responses, posing aesthetic criteria of structure and organization, but analysis of personal responses (reflecting primarily claims of identification) also began to appear. Interestingly, there was also considerable spontaneous consideration of cause and effect, as pupils began to untangle the relationships between the structural characteristics of a work, and the interest or tedium that they felt in reading it. Forty percent of the thirteen-year-olds studied attempted some such untangling, though it did not appear at all in the responses of younger children.[3]

Generalization

The last stage to emerge when adolescents are asked their reasons for liking or not liking stories or poems involves a generali-

Table 5   Children's Criteria in Evaluating Stories and Poems

| | Students Using Once (%) | | | |
| | Comprehensive School | | Selective Schools | |
Type of Criteria	Age 9 (n=30)	Age 13 (n=30)	Age 13 (n=20)	Age 17 (n=20)
Unintegrated	20.0	10.0	10.0	10.0
Categoric	90.0	90.0	90.0	60.0
Analytic	0.0 <	63.3 <	95.0	95.0
Generalizing	0.0 <	26.7	20.0 <	80.0

<   indicates a significant difference at the .05 level, two-tailed, using chi-square tests, $df=1$. See "Tests of Significance," appendix 1.

zation about the meaning or theme of a work, rather than an analysis of its parts. Though both analysis and generalization seem to require the resources of formal operational thought, analysis emerges sooner and more fully in these samples. It may, in fact, have a facilitating role, helping to heighten the reader's sense of the work as consciously structured, and leading toward a consideration of *why* that particular structure was chosen. In any event, we find that analysis occurs alone, but generalization rarely does, usually resting on and elaborating an accompanying analytic base.[4]

When readers at this stage use their subjective, personal responses to justify an evaluation, they concentrate on how the work has interacted with their view of the world: do they understand the world better, have they agreed or disagreed with the author's point of view, or, occasionally, has the work served some specific purpose for them (for example, escape or entertainment)? Keith M. (17 yr 7 mo), for example, likes a story if he can say, "I learned from it"; Nigel L. (17 yr 10 mo) likes it if it is "Relaxing and restful"; Florence G. (13 yr 1 mo) prefers those where "You feel the same way as the author or poet."

When the objective response is used to justify an evaluation at this level, the focus is on the theme of the work, rather than on the reader's own reaction to it. The work's depth, uniqueness, meaningfulness, and relationship to the author or the world in general all become important evaluative criteria. Whereas at the concrete operational level responses focused on *describing* and characterizing content as "types," here the concern is with understanding and explaining them. Charles G. (18 yr 2 mo), for example, rejects a book if it is "pointless," while Lydia M. (18 yr 0 mo) likes those that have an "original theme." Or as Winifred S. (17 yr 5 mo) puts it, linking her personal and objective responses, "Depth of meaning, therefore makes me think."

Such generalization was rare at earlier ages, but was used by some 80 percent of the seventeen-year-olds studied (table 5).

Breadth of Response

The co-occurrence of the different criteria for evaluation is itself an interesting phenomenon. At six and nine, the responses of 64 percent of the children studied were confined to one type; at thirteen, 84 percent used at least two different types (usually, categoric and analytic). By seventeen, the responses of 50 percent reflected three different types (usually, categoric, analytic, and generalizing). This suggests that the modes of thought of the earlier stages are not simply replaced with the new resources of formal operations: children continue to make use of their earlier ability to order and classify, even as they begin to analyze and generalize as well. None of the children at any age used all four types of criteria, reflecting the disappearance of the syncretistic response and of the global but unintegrated "It's good" as sufficient answer.[5]

Levels of Meaning

The shift from simple retelling and summarization by the younger children toward analysis and generalization by the adolescent has at its heart the recognition that a story may operate at more than one level of meaning. Young children's concern with the action suggests that for them a story remains primarily a patterning of events; the early adolescent's ability to analyze reflects the recognition that this pattern has a purpose and conscious ordering; while the generalizations of the older student take the work as implying a broader theme or message. In the last chapter, we saw that preoccupation with concrete action was paralleled with a striking literalism in the interpretation of common sayings and proverbs; not surprisingly, concern with analysis and generalization is paralleled by more complicated interpretations of such sayings.

Nine-, thirteen-, and seventeen-year-olds who responded in writing were asked to explain both "Birds of a feather flock together" and "When the cat is away, the mice will play." For the nine-year-olds, results from these questions were similar to those from the interviews discussed in chapter 6: the majority of children gave a literal interpretation of the action depicted (table 6).[6] The older children studied, however, made use of two new sorts of responses: exemplification and generalization.

Exemplifications are based primarily on analogy, and seem to involve an inference of the form "A is to B as C is to D." For cat and mice, for example, the pupil may substitute teacher and pupils, homeowner and burglars, parents and children. Often this concrete example will be introduced with "It is like when...," with the implication that it is only one of a larger set of possible analogies. Still, the explanation remains tied to one or another specific situation rather than moving to a generalization which would encompass all of them. Gail's response is typical of this type, when she explains the cat and mice with, "When the teacher goes out the children shout" (Gail H., 13 yr 1 mo). So is Elaine's description of birds of a feather: "Bad people stick together and good people stick together" (Elaine G., 14 yr 2 mo).

In contrast with these exemplifications, another set of responses relied on a generalized formulation of meaning. Again, Orlando F. (17 yr 2 mo) is typical of many others when he explains the cat and mice as, "When authority is absent, then the natural order of things begins to break out." Similarly Alice H.

| | Pupils (%) | | | |
| | Comprehensive School | | Selective Schools | |
Explanation	Age 9 (n=30)	Age 13 (n=30)	Age 13 (n=20)	Age 17 (n=20)
Cat and mice				
Don't know	6.7	10.0	5.0	5.0
Literal	86.7	3.3	15.0	5.0
Exemplification	6.7	83.3	70.0	5.0
Generalization	0.0	3.3	10.0	85.0
Birds of a feather				
Don't know	33.3	26.7	15.0	5.0
Literal	60.0	3.3	0.0	0.0
Exemplification	6.7	26.7	50.0	5.0
Generalization	0.0	43.3	35.0	90.0

[a] Age differences in the types of explanations are significant, $p < .005$, for ages nine vs. thirteen, and for thirteen vs. seventeen, using chi-square tests. Differences between the two thirteen-year-old samples are not significant for either saying. On tests of significance, see appendix 1.

(16 yr 5 mo) says of birds of a feather, "Any group of people who have something in common tend to come together for that reason." The shift toward such generalized statements of meaning often loses the vividness and immediacy of exemplification, but carries with it a corresponding gain in efficiency. One formulation of the meaning not only subsumes a whole range of alternative concrete phrasings, but also tends to be much closer to the phrasing that other people use. Still, what is being called exemplification should not be downgraded: the pupils giving this type of answer quite clearly know what it means to use the sayings, and may also have begun to see the meaning in the stories and poems they read and write as embodying a similar concrete abstraction.

The use of these types of response shows very clear age trends (table 6). For the cat and mice saying, by thirteen almost all pupils were giving an exemplification, in both the comprehensive and the selective school settings. By seventeen, this was replaced by an almost universal generalized response. Birds of a feather showed less tendency to lead to exemplification; at thirteen there were more students who gave a generalized answer and also more who did not know what it meant at all. By seventeen, responses to the two sayings again came into balance, with generalized formulations dominating for both.[7]

The intercession of exemplification between the literal interpretation and the fully generalized one may be relevant to the earlier finding that students at thirteen are more likely to use analysis than generalization in discussing stories, even though both operations are dependent on the acquisition of formal operational schemata. The present data suggest that the generalized formulation—which is similar to the problem of formulating discussions of theme or message—is quite difficult, and emerges naturally only after an intermediary stage of relating the statement to other similar situations. This intermediary stage, however, is one which has little equivalent in our traditional modes of discussing literature; rarely, unless we ask for a story or poem in response, do we give students a chance to make this sort of connection between the experience of the work and other experiences with which they may be familiar. We might expect, in fact, that by thirteen they could make such direct analogies relatively easily, but since it is not what they are expected to do in writing about literature, they have not done it spontaneously in the course of answering the present set of questions. If this is the case, then the emergence of analysis without generalization in so many of the essays would not be because the students are analyzing but not generalizing, but because their generalizations are not in a form that they have been encouraged to consider appropriate to written response.[8]

The studies of children's metaphor comprehension introduced in the previous chapter are again relevant here. In the Gardner et al. (1975) study, a completion task provided students with literal, conventional, appropriate, and inappropriate metaphor-completion options. The proportion of appropriate endings chosen rose steadily from ages seven to nineteen, where they were chosen by 53 percent of the sample. Eleven-year-olds showed a greater preference than any other group for conventional endings (71 percent), which decreased gradually to 47 percent by nineteen. A metaphor production task, on the other hand, was dominated by conventional completions from age seven onward; preschoolers had a larger proportion than the other groups of inappropriate endings. More detailed analysis of the reasons given for preferences indicated that the seven- and eleven-year-olds were very concrete and literal in their approach; older children were more analytic, making explicit comparisons between the alternatives offered and sometimes alluding to "middle terms"—"intermediate or relativistic concepts which joined the usually disparate realms."

Billow (1975), after demonstrating that metaphors based on similarity become accessible with concrete operations, went on to indicate that metaphors involving proportionality ("My head is an apple without any core," where head is to apple as brain is to core) become accessible only with the acquisition of the proportionality schema of formal operations. Success in interpreting a series of proverbs included in this phase of the study showed a similar increase with the advent of formal operations, but was not related to success on proportionality-related tasks. Apparently the basis for understanding such sayings lies in a different aspect of formal operational thought.

Beyond the Information Given

We began this chapter by claiming that the major acquisition during adolescence is the ability to move beyond the information given toward a sense of "what might be." In the data we have considered so far, this has manifested itself in two major ways. One has been in the children's new concern with motivational principles—with teasing out cause and effect in the structure of the story, in the actions of the characters, and even in the relationships between objective perceptions of the work and personal, subjective reactions to it. The second manifestation of this concern with "what might be" has been the awareness that a work has implications which transcend the immediate situation —the concern with theme or message or point of view. Essentially, it is the recognition of Harding's (1962) point that a work of fiction is, among other things, "an accepted technique for discussing the chances of life." With this recognition comes an implicit shift of focus, away from the story itself toward the "chances of life" it is discussing.

Such a progression toward a consideration of structure and message has been evident in many previous studies of literary response, though the investigators have not always been aware of the close parallels between the progression in literary response and that found in other domains of thought. These studies have been summarized in Squire (1969), Purves and Beach (1972), D'Arcy (1973), and Applebee (1977); rather than review them again, we will look briefly at two of the most extensive of them, the National Assessment of Educational Progress, and the International Association for the Evaluation of Educational Achievement (IEA) study of achievement in literature.

In addition to the nine-year-old samples discussed in the previous chapter, the National Assessment (1973b) elicited responses from thirteen- and seventeen-year-olds, and from young adults. For all but the nine-year-old sample, written as well as oral responses were gathered for different stories and poems. On all tasks, the results indicated a shift away from "retelling" (which included summary, synopsis, and narrational responses) toward interpretation. This was particularly marked in the results from the written responses, which were categorized globally in a single category rather than analyzed statement by statement. On this task, the percentage of essays categorized as primarily retelling dropped from 44 percent at thirteen to 13 percent at seventeen and 10 percent for the young adults. The proportion categorized as involving primarily interpretation showed a corresponding rise, from 25 percent at thirteen to 71 percent at seventeen and 75 percent for the young adults. Because of the different categorizations used, the results are not directly comparable with the present study, but the movement away from discussion of the action toward analytic, interpretive approaches is still clear.

The IEA study (Purves et al. 1973) involved large samples in nine countries of varied linguistic, educational, and socioeconomic backgrounds.[9] In each country two populations were sampled: fourteen-year-olds and students in their preuniversity year (roughly seventeen, but varying from country to country). One of the instruments used in all countries was a multiple-choice questionnaire which preliminary studies had indicated would provide a reasonably valid and easily scored measure of response preference. Basically, it involved a rating scale of twenty items from which pupils were asked to choose the five questions "that you think are the most appropriate to ask" about a particular story. These choices were then used to build profiles of response preferences.

Of most interest among the many results reported are patterns for the two age groups as they emerged across national boundaries.[10] The investigators noted a "remarkable commonality" in the preference patterns for the preuniversity samples, all of which show a tendency toward formal and thematic responses— or in the terms of the present study, toward analysis and generalization. This is particularly clear in looking at those students who received the highest scores on a separate measure of achievement. The preferences of this group of advanced pupils were (1) "Is there anything in the story that has a hidden meaning?" (chosen by 52 percent); (2) "What emotions does the story arouse in me?" (48 percent); (3) "How can we explain the way the characters behave?" (46 percent); (4) "Is the story about important things? Is it trivial or serious?" (36 percent); and (5) "Is there a lesson to be learned from the story?" (31 percent) (p. 280). All five of these preferred responses involve a movement beyond the information given, to a consideration of motivation and message.

The Implications of the Action

Analysis and generalization are two of the effects of the adolescent's ability to go beyond the information given. A third development has been less evident in the data gathered for the present study: it is the ability to predict what will happen next, either in a story-completion task or in commenting on the effects of the action on characters less directly involved. Such tasks have a common feature: in order to complete them successfully, it is necessary to construct an ongoing representation of the story which will provide a framework for extrapolation. A representation based on either enactive chaining together of incidents or concrete classification of depicted events will not be sufficiently powerful to cope with such a task.

Eliot Freidson's (1953) descriptive analysis of children's responses to television drama is one highly provocative early account of such a development. Studying American children in kindergarten, second, fourth, and sixth grades, he found that for the younger children, "the total plot is weighed only to the extent that it contains incidents that actually elicit excitement." There is little evidence of a structured representation of the stories; the response is "at its most coherent a patchwork of discrete events that are exciting." By fourth grade, the plot has begun to be treated as "combinations of events," whose parts can be contrasted with one another and understood as a set. These are classifications of observed events, however; it is not until sixth grade that Friedson finds evidence of an ability to *predict* what will happen even in highly stylized stories, and the beginning of an extension of this ability to other narrative forms.

Several investigators have studied this ability to draw implications by eliciting responses to incomplete or partially structured story materials. Gardner and Gardner (1971) studied pupils at six, eight, eleven/twelve, and fourteen/fifteen years; each child heard and later completed a story of about 300 words in length, and then repeated it to a second investigator. At that point the whole procedure was repeated, with a second incomplete story in a markedly divergent style. Of more interest to us than the specific age changes reported are the global impressions presented discursively. In particular, the Gardners found that six-year-olds treated stories as though they were comic strips, requiring but one additional line to complete the narrative. These lines were "less inappropriate than incomplete"; they reflected the immediately preceding lines rather than the narrative as a whole. By eight, children interpreted the task "as an occasion to list a long series of events involving a hero. Often these episodes are borrowed from other stories and may be inappropriate. . . ." These responses seem related to concrete operational modes of thought, with the children attempting to satisfy the investigators' demands out of their set of "known endings" to stories; they are still not able to extrapolate beyond the story in a systematic, consistent way. The Gardners were most impressed with the performance of their eleven- and twelve-year-old pupils, who provided endings which were both imaginative and consistent with the drift of the story as a whole. With the oldest sample there was more self-consciousness and uniformity in the renditions offered, which the Gardners suggest may represent a curtailment of literary growth in the face of heightened critical self-awareness. It is possible, however, to interpret this instead as another reflection of the processes underlying the shift from exemplification to generalization in responses to the present study, with the attendant loss of vividness which that shift brings.

Several investigators have concentrated more specifically on the change in ability that comes at adolescence. McCreesh (1970) presented twenty children at nine, thirteen, and fifteen years with descriptive accounts of tragic events in everyday life. He divided the responses into those in which awareness of consequences was restricted to what was actually depicted in the story and those in which it generalized to consequences not portrayed in the story itself. The fifteen-year-olds consistently showed a more generalized awareness in contrast with the nine-year-olds studied, with the thirteen-year-olds varying depending on the specific story with which they were tested. Studies reported by Goldman (1965), Peel (1959), and Case and Collinson (1962) have obtained similar results with biblical, historical, and other narrative material: before about the age of twelve, children show little ability to extrapolate beyond the depicted situation.

All of these studies require the pupil to verbally formulate a response, and leave open the possibility that the child may have a more complete and adequate representation of the story than his or her verbalizations make evident. Thus it is especially interesting to have parallel evidence from nonverbal measures. In an early study DeBoer (1938) measured responses to radio drama by monitoring physiological changes (pulse, blood pressure, respiration, and galvanic skin response) and by recording overt motor reactions at half-minute intervals. He found that young children respond to each incident separately, with no rise or fall of interest over long stretches of the plot. In adolescents, on the other hand, there was a clear development of response over the course of the narrative. This was especially evident with surprise endings: these provoked sharp reactions from adolescents, who had firm expectations about the structure of the story; in younger children who had no such expectations, surprise endings caused no more reaction than any other incident (p. 109). Dysinger and Ruckmick (1933), studying reactions to film using similar physiological measures, have reported similar developmental patterns. Such findings from studies which require no verbalization of response lend added credibility to the assertion that until adolescence, there is little ability to extrapolate beyond the information given, either to complete a narrative with an appropriate (rather than conventional) ending or to answer questions about the effects of the events depicted on characters not so directly involved.

Summary

If we bring together our findings in this and the previous chapter, we have the basis for a systematic model of the major developmental stages in the formulation of response; this model is presented schematically in table 7. At the preoperational stage of intelligence, the characteristic verbal response is to retell the story in whole or in part. There is little sense of the overall structure of the plot, which is treated instead as separate incidents which the child may or may not be able to enactively chain together. At this stage the personal, subjective response seems to lack integration into a coherent and well-organized representation of the experience; syncretism and centration are both very evident.

Table 7   Developmental Stages in the
                               Formulation of Response

Mode of Thinking	Characteristic Response	
	Objective	Subjective
Preoperational (ages 2 to 6)	*Narration*, in whole or part	*Syncretism*, lacking integration
Concrete operational (ages 7 to 11)	*Summarization* and categorization	*Categorization*, attributed to the work
Formal operational stage I (ages 12–15)	*Analysis* of the structure of the work or the motives of the characters; understanding through analogy	*Identification* or perception of involvement in the work
Formal operational stage II (age 16–adult)	*Generalization* about the work; consideration of its theme or point of view	*Understanding* gained or not gained through the work; its effect on the reader's own views

The acquisition of concrete operational schemata, which Piaget places roughly at seven years, brings with it a new ability to summarize and categorize responses, to treat them as representatives of classes. Here both objective and subjective modes of response become important, though the distinction between them is still apparently not recognized by the child. A subjective awareness that a story is "funny" or "exciting" or "sad" is still attributed directly to the work, in the same way that such characteristics as "long," "rhymes," and "love story" may be. In both cases, the child's mental representation or way of construing the work seems to rely on various discrete categories for classifying experiences.

The acquisition of formal operational thought appears to have its influence in two stages. During the earliest of these, probably corresponding to the twelve- to fifteen-year-old age span during which Piaget asserts that these mechanisms are in the process of being acquired, response is formulated as analysis. Though it does not appear in the essays gathered for the present study, other evidence collected suggests that there is also a corresponding tendency toward understanding through analogy or "exemplification": the work is treated as illustrating a much wider class of life experiences. As readers begin to analyze their subjective, personal responses, they also become aware of the distinction between their subjective and objective reactions, tending to formulate the former as identification or involvement; they also tend to begin to look for reasons for their subjective reactions in the objective characteristics of the work.

The second stage of formal operational thought represents the most mature mode of response studied in the course of the present investigation. Here, readers begin to generalize about the meaning of a work, to formulate abstract statements about its theme or message; they seem for the first time to accept it as Harding's "accepted technique for discussing the chances of life." As such, it has taken on a very new role: it is one of many statements of how life might be understood, rather than simply a presentation of life as it is. As part of this awareness, readers' subjective, personal reactions begin to focus on how they, as individuals, have reacted to the work: Have they learned from it? Disagreed with it? Found it clear and satisfying?

Finally, we should note that the stages in the model build on one another. As children mature, they do not pass out of one mode of response into another, but integrate their older structures into a new and more systematic representation of experience. Thus six-year-olds typically have available only the resources of an enactive, often syncretistic and unstructured response. They can retell stories or incidents, but they have yet to develop a stable system of categorization, and they have no way at all to formulate abstract statements about meaning or purpose. Seventeen-year-olds, on the other hand, are typically able not only to generalize, but also to muster the resources of all of the earlier stages. They can analyze in support of their generalizations; they can categorize and summarize; and they can retell in whole or in part, depending on their purpose.

Eight

Reprise

The last five chapters have looked in detail at developmental changes in the relationships between children and stories. In closing, it will be more useful to look again at the value of spectator-role experience than to attempt to recapitulate the detailed findings which have already been highlighted in the individual chapter summaries.

Literature and Experience

Basic to the effect of literature (and of all art) as we have been describing it, is its reliance on Langer's (1967) subjective rather than objective modes of feeling. With transactional uses of language the appeal is to externally structured and verified tools of argument and analysis; with poetic uses, the appeal is to the internal coherence and validity of the personal system of construing. These two modes of language use, like the modes of feeling which underlie them, remain closely and inseparably linked; thus there has been no contradiction in studying literary response through transactional discussions of spectator-role experience.

Transactional or discursive writing has its own range of tasks for which it is especially suited; these have been discussed by others and are not our direct concern here (cf. Britton et al. 1975; Britton 1970; Cassirer, 1944). The poetic mode, however, has its own unique and essential tasks which cannot be slighted if individual and cultural development are to proceed smoothly. Britton (1971*b*) has called the spectator role *assimilative,* and while we need to note that Piaget's processes of assimilation and accommodation are both applicable to spectator-role experience, at another level Britton's description is very much to the point. Assimilation is the way in which new experience is given its meaning; it is a progressive, forward-moving process in that the new experience is in turn incorporated into the framework which assigns that meaning. In this process the world view is primary and focal, whereas in the complementary process of accommodation the events of the world dominate more fully. And the primacy of the world view, the personal representation of experience, is one characteristic of the spectator role as we have been describing it.

It is worth contrasting art as a process of assimilating experience with the view of art as a means to "broaden" or "explore" experience. American progressive educators in particular tended to conceptualize art and literature as offering one or another form of experience; they found in this conceptualization a relatively easy way to defend literature against the ever-present demands of more "practical" subjects (see Applebee 1974). These educators had many valuable insights into literary education, but they lacked a psychological or philosophical framework to give their insights scope and precision. In the end the concern with broadening experience degenerated into a concern with providing vicariously gained knowledge of the world—knowledge that could as easily be gained in other ways.

Any experience, whether it originates in spectator-role uses of language or "in the world," is construed by individuals on their own terms; but there is an essential difference between experience gained through these two means. When we are talking of events in the world, we are talking of events which are unstructured; they are "raw" experience that will be given structure only when they are construed. The structure they are finally given may fit more or less well, may be a full or a partial ordering of experience, but it is a structure which in the first instance does not have to compete with alternative structures offered by other people.

With spectator-role language, on the other hand, there is always a second manner of construing the experience—the manner which makes us talk of the work as a "verbal object" or "structured whole." This structure is a record of the author's processes of construing, a record unconsciously projected into the shaped experience of the work, but governed by accepted techniques of form and structure which allow it to be "read back" by an audience. There is thus a sense in which response in the spectator role is always a process of *re*construing, never simply of construing; there is always another point of view which the auditor is implicitly evaluating even if he or she does not realize it is there. This is the crucial distinction between spectator-role experience and direct experience of the world: the process of construing a text is always a social process in a way that construing primary experience can never be.[1]

Decontextualization

Just as the process of construing experience can be seen as imposing a personal order on it, we can recognize a complementary process in which some part of that order is made public. Britton (1973) has called this a *decontextualization* of experience; it is an abstraction or projection out of our necessarily personal system of construing, our personal context, into a public arena of shared experience. This is the complement of the process of construing; it gives us back both the experience which was initially construed and the structure imposed on that experience in the process of construing. Decontextualization requires the mastery of two very different sets of rules of use for language production, one for the poetic and one for the transactional.

The process of separating our thoughts from the matrix in which they are embedded and making them public through language is very difficult, but it is also very powerful. The speaker or author learns from it just as the audience does, coming to know what he or she thinks as part of the very process of putting it into words. Often, the first words are clearly wrong—the decontextualization produces utterances that imply a view of the world which is not the view the author wants to convey. This is part of the process of drafting and redrafting, of "finding the right words." To the extent that decontextualization is ultimately successful—and this is the paradox in the terminology—the language that results carries the earlier decontextualization or manner of construing within it. If it is "accurate" and "honest," if the rules of language use have been mastered, the discourse invites the audience to share in a part of the author's world.

Whether we are talking about pop music or television comedy, Shakespeare or Albee, it is only through spectator-role discourse that we are able to directly share in aspects of this personal world. It is not that our knowledge of our own world view is relatively imprecise and unformulated, full of unplumbed depths which we approach only hesitantly, if at all; it is because the way in which we construe experience is not organized in the analytic, cumulative forms which are accessible through transactional discourse. At best, in transactional writing we can isolate one strand of our process of construing, analyzing and clarifying its constituent parts; but in the end that transactionally isolated experience must be reintegrated, assimilated, as a functional subsystem within a complex psychological whole.

This is the difference between the objective, analytic response described transactionally by the literary critic and the full, subjective response of the critic or any other reader. In both cases, we have a "reading-back" of meaning from form and structure, but the reader responding subjectively attempts to "operate" the construct system, whereas the critic responding objectively describes and analyzes a part of it. The process of analysis will focus on one or another strand of experience, enriching our understanding and appreciation of it, but it is only when we return to the spectator role and its demands for a personal, subjective reaction that all of the various strands which make up the complex whole can be brought into perspective and balance.

The Elaborative Choice

It is the social process implicit in decontextualization which ultimately is the source of our second dimension of language use. In offering up a point of view, a discourse implicitly assumes a certain relationship between the way it depicts the experience and the generalized patterns of construing expected in its audience: it can seek to change the context from which it stems, leading to a reformulation of the relevant constructs, or it can seek to articulate that context, confirming its essential outline even as it reconciles and explores it in its detail. This is the elaborative choice. For the author, it is a choice of the way in which the presented experience should be assimilated, and the discourse will be structured (not necessarily consciously) toward that end. For the reader, it is a choice of whether to accept or reject the choice the author has made: in the transactional mode the reader judges whether the argument is "right" or "wrong," in the poetic, whether the experience is "consistent" and "convincing." This reaction is a highly personal one, produced by the interaction of the particular reader with the particular work; it inevitably differs from reader to reader and also changes over time as a given reader's construct system develops and matures. A work can lead to a true reformulation only once; after that, it becomes a reference point for the already converted.

Developmental Constraints

These general claims hold across the whole developmental range, though as earlier chapters have demonstrated there are also clear and striking changes in the nature of literary response at different ages. The most fundamental changes seem to center in three areas: (1) the way in which readers perceive the relationship between the experience of the work and their own lives; (2) the extent to which they have mastered the techniques and conventions—the rules of use—of literary form; and (3) the complexity of the experiences (both personal and literary) which they are able to master. Virtually all of the findings which we and others have reported can be subsumed under one or another of these headings, though they serve more to highlight important areas of development than to delineate mutually exclusive ones.

Mastery of conventions and increased complexity are relatively straightforward processes and will not be reviewed again here; the most important findings with respect to both of them have been summarized at the end of the individual chapters. Changes in the perceived relationships between literature and life, however, are striking and influence attitudes toward spectator-role experience in general. For very young children the world of stories is part of the world in which they live; its events are as important and meaningful to them as anything else that happens. The separation of these worlds when they are finally confronted with the distinction between fact and fantasy is often relatively distressing; for a while, at least, a story is accepted only if the child thinks it is true. Slightly older children, once they have reconciled themselves to the distinction between fact and fantasy, continue to view stories from a single perspective: the events in a story remain made-up correlatives of events in the world.

It is not until adolescence, and with it the onset of Piaget's formal operational modes of thought, that spectator-role language begins to be recognized as offering simply a possible view of the world, one among many interpretations. Interestingly, this new perspective often brings a rejection of fantasy similar to that of younger children when they discover that some works are not "true": the early adolescent often rejects works which are not realistic presentations of the world as he or she sees it. Only gradually, as the new perspective on literature becomes more familiar and more thoroughly mastered, are the conventions of fantasy and the possibilities inherent in alternative views of the world accepted freely and openly.

Through all of these stages, the spectator role continues to fulfill its world-ordering functions—more strongly perhaps for younger children who accept the spectator role as offering a view of *the* world than for older students who can set it aside as simply *a* view of the way things are. The experience of the work is no less patterned simply because the young child does not recognize the pattern as yet; it is only through repeated experience with such patterns that stable expectations can eventually be built up.

Because the work functions as a patterning of experience, however, the relationship between literature and life is a complex one. A child's fairy tale, for example, does not simply teach that the world is full of witches and giants. In another sense the tale uses fantasy characters (whom the child will soon enough recognize as "make-believe") to give body and form to the child's worst, shapeless fears—and in the process to begin to conquer them. Just as we use transactional language to give form and precision to our "objective feeling," so we use poetic language to give form, and the possibility of control and precision, to our more subjective, personal feeling. Sometimes in young children this process is unselfconsciously revealed. Barry M. (4 yr 9 mo), in one of the stories in the Pitcher and Prelinger (1963) collection, recounts a tale of a boy whose parents died and who was beset by various tormentors—all ending happily when he "like Hansel and Gretel" pushed them into the oven and "lived happily ever after and that's the end" (pp. 71–72). Such stories offer a culturally provided frame for both expressing and trapping such fears, and through this expression and control freeing the individual from their tyranny. Literature is one of the many instruments of socialization which a culture provides, whether this is thought of in terms of the "cultural heritage" or the popular culture which may be more transient but is no less influential.

Developmental constraints in literary response are in this sense similar to those operating in all areas of socialization: the process begins as what is sometimes called primary socialization, the induction of the child into the accepted modes and conventions of society, and later continues as part of a process of secondary socialization, during which the individual comes to recognize and choose among sometimes conflicting alternatives.

The Teaching of Literature

These discussions have not been concerned directly with the role of the teacher, or of formal education, in the development of literary response, and we are not at this point going to offer an instant prescription about what and how to teach. The discussions do, however, imply a certain attitude toward literature and literary education, an attitude shared by some but certainly not by all teachers.

The main point is that the spectator role offers a way to articulate and explore our view of the world, presenting alternatives, clarifying dark corners, posing contradictions, reconciling conflicts within the realm of our subjective, personal experience. The teacher's role in this process is one of questioning and cultivating response rather than one of teaching critical principles; the goals should be to illuminate and clarify the order in the world which the work seeks to capture and reflect.

Formal studies of literature—concern with rhetorical devices, stanza forms, historical trends—would seem to have little place in this process, but a gradually evolving sense of form is clearly crucial to it. Literary experience depends on the mastery of the underlying conventions which govern the exchange between author and audience; without the conventions no exchange can take place. The source of this sense of form is Britton's (1968) "legacy of past satisfactions," satisfactions which have little to do with training taste or learning rules, and much to do with valuing and being allowed to value those earlier spectator-role experiences which have given pleasure. The patterns of development found in the present study certainly do not suggest that encounters with immature or juvenile literature are any less important, or any less educative, than later encounters with more sophisticated works.

The tasks used in the present study were designed to discover how children naturally respond in their encounters with the spectator role. Looking at the reactions of different age groups to similar tasks has allowed us to trace "developmental stages" in this natural response—stages which suggest at least the direction of growth that can be expected in our work with individual children. What we have not attempted is to look at the *limits* of a child's comprehension and understanding at each age, to find either the level at which frustration ensues, or the performance that can be obtained when the child works in conjunction with a teacher or peer. We need to remember that effective teaching is aimed not so much at the ripe as at the ripening functions—and it is the ripe which we have examined in most detail here. If we heed that caution, the present studies can provide us with a framework for the reformulation of learning in literature and the arts, a framework grounded on the one hand in a view of the place of literature in our lives, and on the other in psychological studies of development in the spectator role.

Appendix One

Collection and Analysis of Data

Introduction

This appendix will be concerned with the technical details of the empirical studies reported in chapters 3 to 7. The first series of studies used a published collection of stories told by children between the ages of two and five (Pitcher and Prelinger 1963). The original investigators analyzed these from a neo-Freudian perspective, using them as a means to explore latent themes or crises of developmental importance. For the present study, analyses concentrated on the stories as a source of information about the expectations which a child has about what a story is, how it is organized, and how it can be "used" or varied in response to different problems.

The second series of investigations was designed to explore age changes in ideas about and responses to literature. At each of the age levels studies, the relatively standard use of structured or semistructured interviews and questionnaires was combined with a parallel exploration using an adaptation of Kelly's (1955) repertory grid technique. The data from interviews and questionnaires are presented in this report; the technically more complex results from the grids have been presented in Applebee (1975, 1976a, 1976b) and in more detail in Applebee (1973a). Copies of all instruments and full scoring instructions are available in Applebee (1973a).

The Analysis of Children's Stories
Subjects

Between 1955 and 1958, Pitcher and Prelinger (1963) collected 360 stories from two-, three-, four-, and five-year-old children in New Haven, Connecticut, and its surrounding communities, in large part from the Gesell Nursery School. Stories were gathered in response to the simple request, "Tell me a story," but children at different ages vary in their willingness to respond to this task. Ames (1966) reports that only about 50 percent of two-year-olds will comply, though by three it is easy to elicit stories.[1] Four-year-olds are again self-conscious and need some coaxing. By five, the major complication is a propensity to retell popular children's tales (*Hansel and Gretel* was the favorite in Pitcher and Prelinger's sample). These retellings are excluded from the collection; when the children had finished them, they were asked, "Now I'd like a story that is your very own, one that nobody else told you, that you made up all by yourself." Pitcher and Prelinger give no data on the proportion of children who did not tell stories at different ages, and none on the interaction between retold and made-up stories when children did both.

The socioeconomic status of the children was uniformly high; almost all were from professional families. In Ames' (1966) sample from the same population, they fall into classes I and II on the Minnesota Parental Occupation Scale. Various IQ and developmental quotients available for the children indicated that 60 percent were of superior ability, 33 percent high average, and only 7 percent average. The children must be assumed to be more articulate and their stories more fully developed than would be the case in a random sample of these ages. The apparent fluency of the stories has probably also been increased by the recording procedure, which relied on transcriptions at the time of storytelling rather than on mechanical recording. Such features as prompting, pausing, and garbled sentences have probably been reduced as a result of the adult mediation. The structure and thematic content of the stories, however, should remain unaffected, as should the direction and nature of changes with age.

Though the population from which the sample is drawn is clear, the sample itself is rather confused. Two stories from each child at two, three, and four are included, and there is a high degree of overlap between the age groups; many children contributed stories during successive years of the study. A subsample of fifteen boys and fifteen girls at each age has therefore been drawn for the present study, eliminating all overlap between year groups and using only the first story told by a child at a particular age. Selection was random within these constraints. The full set of 360 stories was scored, however, and except where otherwise noted showed the same trends as the smaller but statistically more useful subsample.

In the discussion and analysis of data, subjects were cross-classified by age and sex. Both the two- and five-year-old samples are skewed slightly, consisting largely of children between two years six months and two years eleven months in the first case, and less markedly of children between five years and five years six months in the second (table 8).

Scoring Procedures

Pitcher and Prelinger's full sample of stories was randomly numbered and then duplicated with all other identifying information removed. The duplicated stories were ordered on the basis of their assigned random numbers. Scoring was done with related measures scored at intervals to keep them as independent as possible. After scoring was completed, the more subjective scores were recalculated by an independent examiner on a random subsample of twenty-five. Interrater reliability was in general high (see supplementary table 3, appendix 3).

Instruments for the Study of Literary Response
Interviews 1 and 2, and the Reading Questionnaire

Two interview schedules, each taking approximately thirty minutes, were designed for use with six- and nine-year-olds; a parallel "reading questionnaire" was prepared for use with older children. Interviews were tape-recorded, using a portable cassette recorder. Questions focused on various topics of special interest, each with its own series of specific questions scattered through the schedules. Each answer was explored until it seemed certain both that the child had understood the question and that the examiner had understood the response. Rapport was essential and was maintained with standard interviewing techniques. If frustration seemed imminent, leading questions were sometimes used; such "led" responses were not scored.

The areas chosen for investigation emerged from the general literature on child development, especially from Piaget's (1929) work on the child's conception of the world. Particular questions were selected after preliminary work with a vertically grouped

Table 8   Age of Children Telling Stories[a]

	Age Group			
	Two	Three	Four	Five
Boys				
Mean (yr;mo)	2;8	3;6	4;5	5;5
SD (mo)	1.3	2.4	3.2	4.2
Girls				
Mean (yr;mo)	2;8	3;5	4;5	5;4
SD (mo)	2.2	2.9	3.1	3.3

[a] Based on fifteen boys and fifteen girls at each age.

class of five-, six-, and seven-year-olds in southeast London. An informal discussion of this work has been given elsewhere (Applebee 1973*b*).

Major aspects of interview schedule 1 explored children's reasons for liking and for not liking particular stories; their way of discussing a favorite story; expectations about the roles of common story characters and cultural schemata; and understanding of "You must have gotten out of the wrong side of the bed this morning." Interview schedule 2 explored children's understanding of the origin of stories; their sense of the fictional element; their mode of discussing *Little Red Riding Hood*; their ability to retell "The Blind Men and the Elephant"; and their understanding of "When the cat is away, the mice will play."

The reading questionnaire was designed to provide further information on questions which remain relevant at older ages, as well as to gather data on areas of interest only with older students. Here previous investigations of literary response were of more importance; these have been summarized in Squire (1969); Purves and Beach (1972); D'Arcy (1973); and Applebee (1977). A preliminary version of the questionnaire was used with one class each of eleven-, fourteen-, and fifteen-year-olds during the spring of 1972; though these came from one of the schools used in the main study, none of the students participated in both phases.

Repertory Grids

Two orally administered repertory grids (Bannister and Mair 1968) were designed for use in interviews with young children, and two written grids for use with various samples of older ones. One of the oral and one of the written grids was used for the main study of responses to stories; the others were used for a supplementary study of responses to other spectator-role genres and media. The development of these grids, methods of analysis, and results have been reported elsewhere (Applebee 1975, 1976*a*, 1976*b*).

Samples

Piaget's discussions of developmental stages in intellectual growth were used to select target populations likely to show quite different patterns of understanding and response. Six-, nine-, thirteen-, and eighteen-year-old groups were chosen as appropriate school age target populations likely to be biased toward Piaget's preoperational, concrete operational, and early and later formal operational stages. The intent was to maximize the ratio of between- to within-sample variation, not to claim that specific children would have the resources of one or another of these modes of thought available.

To strike a balance between the quality of the data and the amount of time needed to gather it, younger children were individually interviewed but older ones were approached through various written measures. Age nine was used as the changeover point, with samples at that age completing both the written and oral measures.

A single school drawing area was initially chosen for the study, centering on a large comprehensive high school in London, and a nearby set of lower (ages five to seven) and upper (ages eight to eleven) primary schools. A student beginning in the lower school ordinarily moves from there to the upper school, and finally to the comprehensive school; at that stage he or she is joined by students from a number of other similar primary schools. The community as a whole includes a stable working-class population living primarily in postwar public housing. A small proportion of the population are first-generation immigrants, with some bilingualism; pupils for whom English was not the mother tongue were excluded from the population sampled.

Testing was carried out in a five-week period in the autumn of 1972, from mid-September to mid-October. This meant that the eighteen-year-old preuniversity samples were in fact in the seventeen-year-old age band. Work in the various schools and with the various age groups began and continued simultaneously. Though schedules were adjusted to the convenience of the schools rather than rigidly timetabled, the time of day and the day of the week were consciously rotated among age and sex groups.

Interviews with Six- and Nine-Year-Olds

Samples of six- and nine-year-olds were chosen from two schools sharing the same building but with separate administration and staffing. In both schools, children were used from all classes at the selected ages, involving three teachers at each age level. Class lists were used to select pupils at random for testing, with testing terminated after all cells in the design were full. Only pupils in the upper three-quarters of the ability band at each age were interviewed, to insure that the nine-year-olds sampled would be capable of completing the written measures. The final sample of eighty-eight subjects was evenly divided between ages six and nine, between the two interview schedules, and between boys and girls. All of the children in the final sample were in at least their second year of schooling at the time the interviews took place.

The average age of the six-year-old sample was just under six, at five years eleven months (table 9); that of the nine-year-old sample was nine years eight months. Vocabulary as measured by the Mill Hill Vocabulary Scale (Raven 1965) was slightly above average for both age groups, though more so for the girls than for the boys in these samples. (This measure was administered as part of each interview, and scored using Dunsdon and Fraser Roberts' [1955] norms.) Reading scores at nine, based on the Holborn Reading Scale (Watts 1944) administered by each teacher at the beginning of the year, were slightly below average;

Table 9

Age, Reading Ability, and Vocabulary Scores for Children Interviewed[a]

	Age 6 (n=44)	Age 9 (n=44)	Boys (n=44)	Girls (n=44)	Standard Deviation[b]
Age (yr;mo)	5;11	9;8	7;10	7;9	2.9mo
Reading ratio[c]	. . .	95.7	93.8	97.6	15.8
Vocabulary score[d]	104.1	107.1	102.6	108.7	12.8

[a] Analyses of variance indicate no significant differences between the sexes, between the two interview schedules, or for sex by interview interactions for age or for reading achievement. Vocabulary scores show no significant differences for age, interviews, or interactions, but F (sex)$=4.97$; $df=1;80$, $p<.03$.

[b] Pooled within cell.

[c] Reading ratio $=$ (reading age/chronological age) x 100. $N_i=22$, except for the age 9 sample.

[d] Normed mean 100, SD 15, separately for age and sex groups.

differences between reading and vocabulary are more likely due to differing normative samples for the tests than to a within-group discrepancy in achievement in the two areas. In general, the scores suggest that the samples did not deviate strikingly from the average, though there was some constriction in range as a result of the sampling procedure.

Written Measures

The nine-year-old sample for the written measures was simply an extension of that for the interviews. Students receiving the first interview schedule later completed the reading questionnaire; those receiving the second schedule later completed a repertory grid. In both cases, about two weeks elapsed between the interview and the written measures. The sample of sixty pupils was evenly divided between the two measures, and within measures, by sex. There was a twenty-one pupil overlap between interview 1 and the reading questionnaire, and between interview 2 and the written repertory grid. The expansion of the samples to thirty created no significant differences in the scores reported in table 9; final means for the sixty subjects were nine years eight months for age, 106.3 for vocabulary, and 92.7 for reading.

The thirteen-year-old sample was drawn during the same time period from the neighboring secondary school. Sampling was by class, with five classes out of the nine having thirteen-year-olds being used in some phase of the study. Standardized test results were used to select classes biased toward the better students in the school; this bias paralleled that in the nine-year-old sample. The measures were administered during regularly scheduled double-period English classes (approximately ninety minutes); in one case single-period sessions on successive days had to be used. Each session began with a brief description of the study; then the two measures (grid and reading questionnaire) were distributed in alternating order around the class. Students who finished before the period was over were asked to complete the other meas-ure as well, but these second measures were not included in the analyses of results.

In all, forty-five thirteen-year-olds completed the grids as their first measure, and forty-two completed the questionnaire. Ten subjects on the grid and two on the questionnaire left some portion incomplete and were dropped from the analysis. From the remaining pupils, random subsamples of fifteen boys and fifteen girls were drawn for each measure.

The seventeen-year-old population was not successfully sam-pled. After discussions with the staff members involved, these pupils were asked to gather during a free period rather than during a regular class session. Students who came to the sessions cooperated, but very few came—a response which was appar-ently the product of tensions between pupils and some staff members rather than provoked by the study itself. In any event, though some data were gathered the sample was highly self-selected and very small, effectively of very little use.

With the loss of this group it was impossible to draw a seventeen-year-old sample that would be continuous with the three younger groups. Instead of attempting to "match" schools, a new study was set up to investigate changes from thirteen to seventeen in a totally different school situation. For this study, two suburban London single-sex schools with selective admissions were used. Both are long-established, academically oriented schools with large preuniversity classes and some boarding students. Though sharing some facilities, each school has its own history, staff, and financing. New thirteen- and seventeen-year-old samples were drawn at the girls' school during the first week of November and at the boys' school during the last week of November. Procedures were identical with those in the comprehensive school.

At the boys' school, thirty pupils completed the grid and twenty-five the questionnaire as their first measure. From these, ten at each age were randomly drawn for the main analyses of each instrument. At the girls' school, thirty-two subjects completed each instrument, again with a random subsample of ten at each age used for the analyses. In both schools, two teaching groups at seventeen and one at thirteen participated.

Sample Description

Certain further descriptive measures were gathered for the secondary school pupils. Verbal reasoning ability, based on testing just before entry from primary school, was slightly above the London average for the comprehensive school pupils (table 10). On a nationally standardized reading test given to all thirteen-year-olds the previous spring, these classes had an average score of 107 (normed mean 100, SD 15).

Social class and socioeconomic status were estimated from data on parents' occupations gathered on a background information questionnaire. No pressure was put on students to complete this item, and there was some resistance to it in the comprehensive school where some of the parents were unemployed; nonetheless the majority responded as requested. Occupations were then classified into the categories in table 11. The parents of the comprehensive school children tended to be skilled workers, with very few families falling either into the "professional" or the "unskilled" social class groups; in terms of socioeconomic

Table 10   Age, Verbal Reasoning Ability, and
                                                Estimates of Own Reading for
                                                Secondary School Students

	Comprehensive	Selective	
	Age 13 (n=60)	Age 13 (n=40)	Age 17 (n=40)
Age (yr;mo)	13;8	13;7	17;6
SD (mo)	3.5	4.3	6.5
Verbal reasoning	110.2	...	...
SD	15.5		
Books read in past month	3.7	6.9	4.8
SD	3.4	6.7	3.8

status, they represented the two somewhat disparate groupings
of junior and intermediate nonmanual workers (for example,
clerks, typists, salesmen) and skilled or semiskilled manual
workers (carpenters, bricklayers, taxi drivers). Though occupa-
tional data were not available for the parents of the six- and
nine-year-olds, the area is homogeneous and stable enough to
expect little difference. Parents of the selective school children,
on the other hand, were primarily professionals (for example,
doctors, lawyers, teachers) and business leaders.

Treatment of Data
Scoring Interviews and Questionnaires

All scoring and analysis was done by the investigator, with independent checks on scoring consistency and category definitions.
Interviews were scored directly from tape recordings; interviews
from the two age and two sex groups were interspersed, but the
source of each interview was known at the time of coding.

Written responses were coded in random order after deletion
of information about age and class membership; because of time
scheduling in the study as a whole the comprehensive and selective school samples were scored separately in the initial analyses.

Table 11   Social Class of Secondary School Students[a]

Social Class	Comprehensive[b] (%) (n=120)	Selective (%) (n=80)
I. Professional	1.7	42.5
II. Intermediate	14.2	31.3
III. Skilled	35.8	7.5
IV. Partly skilled	15.8	0.0
V. Unskilled	0.8	0.0
Other[c]	31.7	18.8
Total	100.0	100.0

[a] Procedures and category definitions as specified in General Registry Office (1966), which is compatible with International Labor Office (1958) recommendations.

[b] This includes sixty pupils who participated in a supplementary study of responses to other genres and media.

[c] "Other" includes unemployed, unclassifiably vague descriptions, and students who did not respond.

Scoring categories were defined in advance and expanded with full rescoring when heterogeneity among the responses seemed to be obscured; empty or low frequency categories were combined during the statistical analyses.

Discussions of a favorite story and of a story known well were divided into T-units (Hunt 1965) and scored using the Purves-Rippere (1968) coding system. These analyses are reported in appendix 2. Scoring consistency was computed by having a sample of 100 T-units (one selected randomly from each of the discussions) independently rescored. This yielded 63 percent agreement in coding the 139 elements, 76 percent in coding the 24 subcategories, and 81 percent in coding the 5 main categories. These are within the range of agreement between pairs of raters reported by Purves and Rippere (1968) for some of their own studies.

After the initial analyses had been completed on the basis of this scoring system, the reanalyses reported in chapters 6 and 7 were undertaken. For these, the essays were rescored in random order, with comprehensive and selective school samples pooled.

Tests of Significance

Categorical data were analyzed using the SPSS system (Nie et al. 1970, 1975) as implemented at the University of London Computer Center on its CDC 6600 computer. Parametric analyses were carried out using MANOVA (Bock 1963; Bock and Haggard 1968) and the BMD series (Dixon 1968, 1970), again as implemented at the University of London Computer Center. All three provide widely used and well-documented routines for various standard statistical procedures.

These systems were supplemented by hand calculations for some simple effects. Fisher's exact test was computed using Siegel's (1956) tables for those cases where frequencies in all cells were greater than 1; exact levels were used in other cases. Interactions in two-by-two tables in which the entries are proportions of a third variable were also tested by hand, using an approximate test based on the normal distribution. Snedecor and Cochran (1967) discuss this test using an arcsin transformation in degrees; Langer and Abelson (1972) have discussed it using radians.

Frequency distributions were obtained for all categorical variables, and adjacent or related categories combined as suggested by Cochran for appropriate use of chi-square as a test statistic. Cochran's criteria are summarized in Snedecor and Cochran (1967) and more conservatively in Siegel (1956). For two-by-two tables, calculations of chi-square included a correction for continuity; cf. Siegel (1956) or Snedecor and Cochran (1967).

For the children's stories, summed scores were computed within series of highly related variables to provide some control for the multiple comparisons involved. These were dichotomized or used in analyses of variance as their distributions warranted. Age and sex differences were tested for all measures; for variables which could be treated as representing underlying interval scales these included tests of interactions. For most of the categorical data, only main effects were tested, using chi-squares on the appropriate bivariate distributions.

The design of the study of six- to seventeen-year-olds, with the change from oral to written measures at age nine and from the comprehensive to the selective school setting at age thirteen, makes overall tests of significance of questionable value and validity. Instead, both univariate and multivariate analyses have been limited to the contrasts between adjacent ages, between school settings, and between oral and written responses to similar questions. Sex differences have been tested within these constraints. In reporting results, the nine- and thirteen-year-old samples from the London primary school and its associated comprehensive school have been discussed as a single "comprehensive school" population. Similarly, the two selective schools have been treated as one population. Sex and interaction effects have been tested for the selective school samples, though they confound a between-school effect with any sex differences.

To help untangle the various samples and instruments in the study as a whole, supplementary table 1 in appendix 3 provides a brief summary of the overall design.

Appendix Two

The Elements
of Response

Analyzing Response

Collecting discussions of stories such as those reported in chapters 6 and 7 is time-consuming but straightforward; quantifying the responses in a meaningful way is both time-consuming and difficult. Various systems of analysis have been proposed in previous research, but they have been eclectic, resulting from content analysis of obtained responses and the more or less intuitive sense of the investigator about which varieties are "interesting" or "related." These studies have been summarized by Squire (1969), Purves and Beach (1972), and D'Arcy (1973); they provide a background of experience and expectations out of which the present study developed.

In addition to the analyses reported earlier, the present study also made use of a set of "elements" of response developed by Purves and Rippere (1968) as a neutral, atheoretical means of describing literary reactions by coding them statement by statement. These elements range from such literary devices as "allusion" and "irony" to general statements of "thematic importance" or "identification"—139 elements in all, combined into 24 subcategories and 5 categories.

Purves and Rippere based their ordering primarily though not exclusively on traditional forms of literary criticism, but this is not made explicit and leaves the results ambiguous. Having found changes in patterns of response, we are left with the question of just what these changes represent. In spite of this problem, the elements provide the most thorough system of content analysis yet proposed for literary response, and have been quite widely adopted by other investigators. (A recent review found thirty reported studies using the elements, including two large-scale investigations and a host of doctoral studies; cf. Applebee, 1977.) Though the elements were developed on the basis of samples of response from secondary school children, and might be expected to be less satisfactory with our two youngest samples, all responses were initially scored using them. This provided a starting point in the development of the system of analysis reported in chapters 6 and 7. Since the elements themselves have been so popular, however, the preliminary data may also be of interest to other investigators, and will be discussed in this appendix.

To summarize the five major categories in the Purves-Rippere system very briefly, the first is "Engagement-Involvement" and reflects the "suspension of disbelief" or "identification" which the reader acknowledges. The second category is "Perception"; this is the way the reader perceives the work as an objective construct. It includes analysis and classification of the work as well as description of the plot. The third category is "Interpretation," the drawing of inferences about either content or form; where perception is based in the characteristics of the work, interpretation involves a generalization beyond it. The fourth category is "Evaluation," how the reader judges the effect, the style, or the importance of a work. Finally a fifth category is used for miscellaneous digressions and unscorable responses.

Results

At six, three boys and three girls who wanted to retell the story gave up because they "didn't remember it well enough." These refusals (which fall almost entirely in the "miscellaneous" response category) are not included in the calculations which follow.

When the discussions were divided into T-units (Hunt 1965) and classified using this system of analysis, there were no systematic changes in the use of the five main response categories from six to thirteen. Through the age of thirteen, responses classified as perception accounted for 70 percent or more of each answer, with virtually no interpretation and a fluctuating percentage of evaluation. Between thirteen and seventeen, the proportion of responses classified as perception dropped to 31 percent, with a rise in interpretation to 19 percent and evaluation to 38 percent. (These data are summarized more fully in supplementary table 11, appendix 3.) Such changes are in line with those found in other investigations (see Applebee, 1977).[1]

Variety and Complexity

Analysis in terms of the five major categories could obscure differences occurring in the subcategories and elements, but that is not the case here. The general pattern found was for each subcategory and each element, whatever more general category it might belong to, to be used in a higher proportion of the older students' responses. Out of all twenty-four subcategories, for example, only that labeled "content" showed a decrease with age; it was used by 94 percent of the children at six, but only 55 percent at seventeen. This unique decrease resulted from the movement away from simple retelling and summarizing.

The lack of differences in the responses of six-, nine-, and thirteen-year-olds when scored with the Purves-Rippere (1968) system was one of the initial reasons for developing the system of analysis reported in chapter 6. Essentially, the changes of developmental interest were occurring within the element "action," rather than in the balance between this and other elements in the scoring system.

The general rise in the use of each element of response reflects the tendency of older children to produce a more complex answer, acknowledging a variety of aspects of a story rather than concentrating on the plot or the characters or the theme alone. Though the six-year-olds' discussions are longer, on the average, than those of any other group, they typically draw on only 1.3 different elements of response; by seventeen, this has risen to 5.5. There is a discontinuity introduced by the shift from oral to written responses at age nine, but this disappears if the lengths are roughly equated: the average number of repetitions of each element used falls steadily, from twenty-seven at six to just over one at seventeen (supplementary table 12, appendix 3). During the same period, the average number of words per T-unit increases, reflecting the more complex linguistic structures which the older children use.

At age nine, the oral responses are significantly longer than the written ones. Interestingly, however, the added difficulty of the written task may be inducing a more mature response in some pupils: the written responses are linguistically more complex as measured by the average number of words per T-unit, and show some evidence of greater complexity as measured by the average number of T-units per Purves-Rippere element. Using t-tests of within-pupil differences for the twenty-one subjects who completed both tasks, the first four variables in supplementary table 12 show significant differences between oral and written responses at the .02 level or better, the last, at the .08 level, all two-tailed.

Most Important Response

After writing about the story they had chosen, children were asked to indicate the part of their answer which they thought represented the most important thing to say about the story. These responses paralleled the findings already reported: the nine-year-olds overwhelmingly chose some aspect of the action as the most important part (66.7 percent); another 17 percent indicated some form of evaluation. By thirteen, concern with action dropped to 53.3 percent in the comprehensive school and 45 percent in the selective schools, with evaluation at 26.7 and 20 percent, respectively. By seventeen, none selected action as most important, 45 percent chose an evaluative response, and the remainder scattered between interpretation (25 percent), engagement (10 percent), and aspects of structure, genre, or tone (20 percent altogether).

Appendix Three

Supplementary Tables

Supplementary Table 1 Summary of Major Instruments and Samples, Ages Six to Seventeen[a]

	Instruments Used with Each Sample												
School	Lower Primary		Upper Primary		Comprehensive School					Selective Schools			
Age	6		9		11	13			16	13		17	
Sample[b]	A	B	A	B	C	A	B	C	C	A	B	A	B
Sample size	22	22	31	31[c]	20	30	30	20	20	20	20	20	20
Main study													
Interview 1	x		x										
Interview 2		x		x									
Questionnaire			x				x			x		x	
Oral grid	x		x										
Written grid				x			x				x		x
Supplementary study													
Oral grid		x		x									
Written grid					x			x	x				
Background													
Questionnaire					x	x	x	x	x	x	x	x	x
Vocabulary scale	x	x	x	x									
Reading scale			x	x									

a Results from the grids in the main and supplementary studies are reported in Applebee (1975, 1976*a, b*).

b A and B samples are drawn from the same class groups.

c N=22 for interviews and oral grids, 30 for written measures, with a twenty-one-pupil overlap between the oral and written measures.

Supplementary Table 2 Five Most Frequently Cited Titles at Each Age[a]

Age 6 (out of 154 titles)

13	*Jack and Jill*
9	*Baa Baa Black Sheep*
9	*Cinderella*
8	*Humpty Dumpty*
7	*Goldilocks*

Age 9 (out of 484 titles)

20	*The Three Little Pigs*
12	*Bedknobs and Broomsticks*
12	*The Lion, the Witch, and the Wardrobe*
12	*Sleeping Beauty*
11	*The Princess and the Pea*
11	*Snow White*

Age 13, Comprehensive School (out of 440 titles)

22	*Escape on Monday*
20	*Of Mice and Men*
16	*The Hobbit*
16	*Walkabout*
8	*The Lion, the Witch, and the Wardrobe*
8	*The Silver Sword*
8	*Skinhead*

Age 13, Selective Schools (out of 250 titles)

8	*Love Story*
7	*Pilgrim's Progress*
6	*Gone with the Wind*
6	*Lord of the Rings*
5	*The Snow Goose*

Age 17, Selective Schools (out of 250 titles)

12	*Lord of the Rings*
9	*Sons and Lovers*
9	*1984*
7	*Lord of the Flies*
6	*The Go-Between*
6	*Hard Times*

---

a Pooling results from all instruments, including the repertory grids. In the study as a whole, pupils were asked to nominate a total of 1,772 titles. In response, they named 796 specific, different titles and 63 specific, different series (for example, Batman). Another 38 responses gave a general category (ghost stories, for example) or a collection (such as *Five Great Tales of Action and Adventure*); 7 cited stories by a specific author; 20 responded without indicating a specific title (for example, "poems are usually ..."); and 22 gave no response. •

Supplementary Table 3 Interrater Reliabilities for Selected Measures[a]

Measure	Agreement (%)	Pearson Correlation	Cramer's V
Use of formal opening	100.0	...	...
Use of formal closing	100.0	...	...
Number of distinct characters	...	.85	...
Number of distinct incidents	...	.80	...
Degree of fantasy in characters	60.0	.60	
Degree of fantasy in actions	56.0	.18	.36
Degree of fantasy in setting	60.0	.62	.57
Social acceptability of action depicted	80.0	.78	.74
Type of climax	60.0	...	.60
Type of plot structure	44.0	.57	.52
Unity through			
Keeping one character throughout story	96.0	...	.85
Keeping one type of action	68.0	...	.32
Keeping story to single incident	60.0	...	.39
Keeping story to single setting	76.0	...	.58
Keeping story to single theme	100.0	...	...

[a] Estimates are based on a random subsample of twenty-five stories scored by an independent examiner. On Cramer's V as a nonparametric measure of association, see Nie et al. (1970, 1975).

Supplementary Table 4

Use of Formal Elements of Story Form

| | Children (%) | | | | |
Element	Age 2 (n=30)	Age 3 (n=30)	Age 4 (n=30)	Age 5 (n=30)	Chi-square[a] (df=3)
1. Formal beginning	30.0	43.3	76.7	86.7	26.87***
2. Formal ending	0.0	13.3	13.3	46.7	23.82***
3. Consistent past tense	63.3	80.0	93.3	86.7	9.63*
Summed score mean	.93	1.37	1.83	2.20	$p < .001$[b]

[a] Test of age differences. There were no significant differences between the sexes using chi-squares with ages pooled for variables 1 to 3.

[b] Two-factor analysis of variance, linear age effects, $F = 43.49$, $df = 1;112$; *ns* for higher-order age effects, sex, and interactions.

* $p < .05$.

*** $p < .005$.

Supplementary Table 5

Knowledge of Common Story Characters

	Children (%)[a]		
Character	Age 6 (n=22)	Age 9 (n=22)	Chi-square[b] (df=1)
1. Lion	27.2	40.9	5.83**
2. Wolf	54.5	77.3	1.62
3. Rabbit	13.6	59.1	7.96***
4. Fox	4.5	63.6	14.57***
5. Fairy	9.1	50.0	6.99***
6. Witch	22.7	77.3	11.00***
7. Three or more of the above	40.9	86.4	7.96***
8. Boy's pet	45.5	81.8	4.81**
9. Girl's pet	31.8	77.3	7.43***

[a] For categories 1 through 7, the percentages are of children above the median in knowledge of each role. The data are not comparably scaled and cannot be used to determine, for example, whether a "fox" or a "wolf" has a more firmly defined role for these children. For category 8, the percentages are of children reporting that a boy in a story usually has a dog (and only a dog) for a pet; for category 9, the percentages are of children reporting that a girl usually has a cat (and only a cat) for a pet.

[b] Test of age differences. For categories 1 through 7, this is a median test; for categories 8 and 9 the ordinary chi-square. There were no significant differences between the sexes using chi-square tests for main effects, $df=1$, two-tailed.

** $p < .01$.

*** $p < .005$.

	Averages				
Measure	Age 2 (n=30)	Age 3 (n=30)	Age 4 (n=30)	Age 5 (n=30)	F-Statistics[a] (df=1;112)
Number of words	31.0	75.2	110.0	218.9	94.43***
Number of T-units	6.0	10.7	13.0	28.3	105.85***
Words per T-unit	5.3	7.3	8.1	7.7	39.64***
Number of characters	2.1	3.9	3.4	5.4	28.45***
Number of incidents	3.2	4.2	4.3	7.4	22.36***

[a] Test of linear age effects from two-factor (age x sex) analysis of variance. A multivariate analysis of variance for the five measures yielded F (age linear)=42.06 ($p<.005$); F (age quadratic)= 5.95 ($p<.005$); F (age cubic)= 4.67 ($p<.005$). All sex and interaction effects, *ns*. Degrees of freedom for all multivariate effects=5;108. Predicted intervals between ages were based on average age in months for each group.

*** $p<.005$.

1. One consistent character
2. Similar action throughout
3. Single incident
4. Constant setting
5. Thematic center
6. Causal links
    Some
    Clear
7. Climax of action
    Natural
    Thematic
8. High use of fantasy[c]
9. High use of formal markers

---

10. Number of words
11. Number of T-units
12. Number of characters
13. Number of incidents
14. Words per T-unit

---

[a] For variables 1 to 5, narratives and focused chains are contrasted with the four simpler types; for all other variables, the six plot structures are considered separately.

[b] Fisher's exact test (Siegel 1956).

[c] See discussion in chapter 5 of fantasy in characters, action, and setting. This is a summed score, dichotomized at the median.

[d] A multivariate analysis of covariance, variables 10 through 14, yielded two significant roots: F $(25;406.4) = 2.64$, $p < .001$; and F $(16;364.5) = 2.19$, $p < .005$.

		Plot Structures Showing Listed Characteristic (%)					
Heaps (n=10)	Sequences (n=27)	Primitive Narratives (n=17)	Unfocused Chains (n=10)	Focused Chains (n=48)	Narratives (n=8)	df	Chi-square[a]
60.0	92.6	94.1	30.0	97.9	100.0	1	9.26***
20.0	51.9	70.6	50.0	35.4	37.4	1	2.43
50.0	7.4	47.1	10.0	10.4	12.5	1	3.17
60.0	48.1	64.7	50.0	29.2	50.0	1	5.28*
10.0	0.0	0.0	0.0	4.2	25.0	1	ns[b]
20.0	18.5	29.4	70.0	37.5	12.5		
10.0	0.0	52.9	30.0	52.1	87.5	10	69.88***
10.0	14.8	17.6	10.0	22.9	12.5		
0.0	14.8	11.8	20.0	20.8	75.0	10	21.98*
0.0	37.0	5.9	70.0	45.8	87.5	5	27.12***
10.0	48.1	23.5	70.0	64.6	100.0	5	24.46***
		Averages				Covariance on Age[d] F-Statistics (df=5;113)	
57.5	60.6	55.6	154.5	135.6	255.8	2.68*	
8.0	9.2	7.8	20.5	17.6	28.6	1.98	
4.3	2.5	3.0	6.7	3.6	5.2	4.47***	
2.9	4.9	2.9	5.2	5.3	6.3	1.05	
7.0	6.2	7.1	7.3	7.4	8.9	1.37	

Without covariance, all variables show significant differences between plot structures.

* $p < .05$.

*** $p < .005$.

Supplementary Table 8

Measure of Distancing

1. Characters
   Realistic
   Mixed
   Fantasy

2. Self excluded from story

3. Action
   Realistic
   Mixed
   Fantasy

4. Setting
   Realistic
   Mixed
   Fantasy

5. Fantasy total score: mean[b]

	Children (%)					Age Contrasts		Sex Contrasts	
Age 2 (n=30)	Age 3 (n=30)	Age 4 (n=30)	Age 5 (n=30)	Boys (n=60)	Girls (n=60)	df	Chi-square	df	Chi-square
70.0	36.7	60.0	36.7	48.3	53.3	3	7.16	1	0.97
3.3	20.5	3.3	10.0	11.7	6.7		[Fantasy vs. realistic]		
26.7	43.3	36.7	53.3	40.0	40.0				
90.0	80.0	90.0	96.3	93.3	85.0	1	1.39a	1	1.38
76.7	30.0	26.7	6.7	26.7	43.4	6	40.06***	2	9.89**
16.7	53.3	60.0	53.3	43.3	48.3				
6.7	16.7	13.3	40.0	30.0	8.3				
96.7	56.7	76.7	33.3	53.3	78.3	6	30.44***	2	8.69**
0.0	16.7	13.3	23.3	16.7	10.0				
3.3	26.7	10.0	43.3	30.0	11.7				
.93	2.63	1.97	3.60	2.72	1.85		$p < .001$		$p < .008$

a Contrasting ages 2 and 3 with ages 4 and 5.

b Sum of variables 1, 2, and 4. Probabilities from two-factor (age x sex) analysis of variance. F (linear age)$=25.51$; F (quadratic age)$= 0.01$; F (cubic age)$= 11.42$; F (sex)$= 7.34$; F (interactions)$= 1.17$; $df = 1;112$ for main effects, $3;112$ for interactions.

** $p < .01$.

*** $p < .005$.

Status of Action	Stories (%)			Tests of Effects[a]	
	Accept-able	Sanc-tioned[b]	Not Ac-ceptable	Acceptable vs. Others	Interaction Age by Action
N (younger)[c]	18	26	16	Chi-square	
N (older)[c]	16	19	25	$df=1$	Z
Realistic characters					
Younger	61.1	50.0	50.0	0.26	0.86
Older	43.8	42.1	56.0	0.02	
Realistic setting					
Younger	94.4	69.2	68.8	3.23*	0.16
Older	81.3	42.1	48.0	4.71*	
Self excluded					
Younger	61.1	100.0	87.5	8.99***	3.12***
Older	100.0	89.5	92.0	0.44	
Consistent past tense					
Younger	44.4	84.6	81.3	7.57***	2.53*
Older	93.8	84.2	92.0	0.01	
Formal beginning					
Younger	33.3	30.8	50.0	0.00	0.22
Older	81.3	78.9	84.0	0.11	
Formal closing					
Younger	11.1	7.7	0.0	0.12	0.05
Older	37.5	26.3	28.0	0.20	

[a] One-tailed for main effects, two-tailed for interactions. On the test of interactions, see appendix 1, "Tests of Significance."

[b] Sanctioned includes sickness, injury, and conventional violence.

[c] Younger: 2 yr 0 mo–3 yr 11 mo; older: 4 yr 0 mo–5 yr 11 mo.

* $p < .05$.

*** $p < .005$.

Supplementary Table 10   Formal Characteristics of Discussions of Stories

	Children (%)						
	Retelling		Any Synopsis		Any Summary		
	Fav.	*LRRH*	Fav.	*LRRH*	Fav.	*LRRH*	
Characteristic	(n=15)	(n=12)	(n=17)	(n=18)	(n=6)	(n=13)	Chi-square[a]
1. Tense							
Past	100.0	91.7	76.5	0.0	0.0	15.4	37.30***
Mixed[b]	...	8.3	...	27.8	...	7.7	(*df*=2)
Present	0.0	0.0	23.5	72.2	100.0	76.9	
2. Formal opening	60.0	8.3	11.8	0.0	0.0	0.0	13.32*** (*df*=1)
3. Formal closing	40.0	8.3	0.0	11.1	0.0	0.0	6.89** (*df*=1)
4. Dialogue							
Quoted	93.3	83.3	17.6	11.1	0.0	7.7	47.13***
Described[c]	...	0.0	...	44.4	...	0.0	(*df*=2)
None	6.7	16.7	82.4	44.4	100.0	92.3	
	Averages						
5. Number of words	248.1	145.5	184.0	80.0	43.3	24.5	
6. Number of T-units	37.8	19.6	21.7	9.8	6.1	4.0	
7. Words per T-unit	6.6	7.7	8.3	8.1	6.6	6.0	

Multivariate Analysis of Variance for Variables 5, 6, and 7			
Effect[d]	*df*	F-Statistic	Univariate Effects (.05)
Discussion type			
Root 1	6;136	12.56***	5,6,7
Root 2	2;68.5	5.82***	
Story (*Little Red Riding Hood* vs. favorite)	3;68	8.50***	5,6
Interaction			
Root 1	6;136	3.16***	6
Root 2	2;68.5	2.82	

a Test of difference between types of discussion, pooling results from *Little Red Riding Hood* (*LRRH*) and a favorite story. Categories combined to raise expected frequencies to appropriate levels: for tense, mixed + present; for opening and closing, synopsis + summary; for dialogue, described + none. (Cf. appendix 1, "Tests of Significance.")

b For favorite stories, discussions which included a mix of past and present were scored as present.

c For favorite stories, dialogue which was described but not quoted directly was scored as none.

d Because cell sizes are not proportional, these effects are not orthogonal. Each effect is tested after allowing for the influence of the other effects. Since there are three categories for types of discussion, the multivariate test has two independent roots for the corresponding effects.

** $p < .01$.

*** $p < .005$.

Supplementary Table 11   Purves-Rippere Categories in
                                    Discussions of Stories

| | Favorite Story Interviews | | Story Known Well | | | |
| | | | Comprehensive School | | Selective Schools | |
Category	Age 6 (n=16)[a]	Age 9 (n=22)	Age 9 (n=30)	Age 13 (n=30)	Age 13 (n=20)	Age 17 (n=20)
1. Engagement	0.0	2.8	0.0	0.8	3.2	6.6
2. Perception	92.9	78.0	71.1	79.0	71.8	31.3
3. Interpretation	0.4	0.5	0.0	3.6	4.2	19.3
4. Evaluation	6.3	16.0	23.1	14.3	17.4	38.1
5. Miscellaneous	0.4	2.8	5.8	2.4	3.4	4.7

	6 vs. 9	9 vs. 13	13 vs. 13	13 vs. 17
	Multivariate F-statistics[b]			
Age (or school)	0.64	1.48	0.42	6.06***
Sex[c]	0.68	1.48	2.38	4.15**
Interactions[d]	1.03	0.57	1.06	2.87*
(df for each effect)	(4;31)	(4;53)	(4;43)	(4;33)
	Significant (.05) Univariate Effects			
Age (or school)	. . .	. . .	. . .	2,3,4
Sex	. . .	. . .	2,5	2,5
Interactions	. . .	. . .	. . .	1

[a] Sample omits three girls and three boys who did not respond.

[b] Since there is a linear dependency in the scores, multivariate analyses are based on only four variables; results are identical whichever one is omitted. Univariate effects are listed only if the multivariate F reaches at least the .20 level of significance.

[c] In the selective school sample, girls give more perception responses and fewer miscellaneous ones than boys give.

[d] In the selective school sample, at thirteen engagement averaged 5.4 percent for the boys and 1.1 percent for the girls; at seventeen, engagement averaged 0.0 percent for the boys and 13.2 percent for the girls.

* $p < .05$.

** $p < .01$.

*** $p < .005$.

Supplementary Table 12 Length and Variety in Discussions of Stories

	Average					
	Interviews		Comprehensive School		Selective Schools	
Measure	Age 6 (n=16)	Age 9 (n=22)	Age 9 (n=30)	Age 13 (n=30)	Age 13 (n=20)	Age 17 (n=20)
1. Number of words	193.2	124.5	52.6	91.2	120.8	114.7
2. Number of T-units	29.5	15.5	5.6	8.4	9.3	6.8
3. Words per T-unit	6.4	7.1	9.4	11.8	13.6	17.7
4. Number of elements[a]	1.3	2.2	1.5	3.3	4.1	5.5
5. T-units per element	27.4	9.7	4.5	2.9	3.4	1.2

	6 vs. 9	9 vs. 13	13 vs. 13	13 vs. 17
	Multivariate F-Statistics			
Age (or school)	5.10***	9.32	2.46*	3.00*
Sex[b]	1.28	1.50	3.06*	1.59
Interaction[c]	1.22	2.44*	1.28	0.53
(df for each effect)	(5;30)	(5;30)	(5;42)	(5;32)
	Significant (.05) Univariate Effects			
Age (or school)	2,4,5	1,4,3	. . .	3,5
Sex	. . .	. . .	1,2,5	. . .
Interaction	. . .	3	. . .	. . .

[a] Number of Purves-Rippere (1968) elements of response used at least once by each pupil.

[b] In the two thirteen-year-old samples, the girls use more words and more T-units, and have a higher T-unit per element ratio, than do the boys.

[c] In the comprehensive school sample, the girls use more words per T-unit than the boys at nine, and fewer than the boys at thirteen.

* $p < .05$.

*** $p < .005$

Chapter One

1. Piaget's publications are so numerous that general statements about his theory in this and later chapters will not attempt to enumerate them. As a convenient summary and bibliography, Flavell's (1963) analysis will serve for most purposes.
2. This is one of many points where the various traditions of theory and research which we are drawing on show striking convergences. Thus Karmiloff-Smith and Inhelder (1975), continuing Piaget's work, note: "The tendency to explain phenomena by a unified theory, the most general or simplest one possible, appears to be a natural aspect of the creative process, both for the child and the scientist."
3. The terminology here is taken from the work of Jerome Bruner and his colleagues. Cf. Bruner (1974) for a comprehensive introduction and bibliography.
4. Cf. Berger and Luckmann (1966): "My and his 'here and now' continuously impinge on each other as long as the face-to-face situation continues. As a result, there is a continuous interchange of my expressivity and his. I see him smile, then react to my frown by stopping the smile, then smiling again as I smile, and so on. Every expression of mine is oriented toward him, and vice-versa, and this continuous reciprocity of expressive acts is simultaneously available to both of us. This means that, in the face-to-face situation, the other's subjectivity is available to me through a maximum of symptoms.... All other forms of relating to the other are, in varying degrees, remote" (pp. 28–29).

Chapter Two

1. We will develop the model with respect to language, since that is our primary concern in this book. It generalizes readily, however, to other systems of symbolic representation. See Applebee (1976c).
2. James Moffett (1968) has argued that the continuum of transactional techniques can be seen as a succession of different "logics," each of which has its own rules. This is much to our point, though we want to emphasize that each "logic" is in effect a system of representation and must be taken to include all of the special conventions and rules of procedure of the particular professional discipline.
3. Thus Polanyi (1958): "Since the formal affirmations of a theory are unaffected by the state of the person accepting it, theories may be constructed without regard to one's normal approach to experience" (p. 4). Theories in his sense here are equivalent to transactional representations of experience.
4. Frye (1957) has commented on our lack of a good word to describe a work of literary art, pointing out that one "may invoke the authority of Aristotle for using 'poem' in this sense." But he goes on to declare, "a poem is a composition in metre, and to speak of *Tom Jones* as

a poem would be an abuse of ordinary language" (p. 71). We find ourselves in somewhat the same difficulty, ameliorated only somewhat by our focus on techniques of symbolization rather than naming of genres.

5. Kenneth Burke (1945) has given particular attention to the way in which such larger units are handled, noting for example that the "name of any well-developed character in fiction is the term for a peculiar complex of motives" (p. 33); these units can then be balanced against one another in much the same way that smaller units are in a short poem.

6. The notions of participant and spectator have been developed most fully by James Britton (1970), who has also used them to structure the work of the Writing Research Unit at the University of London Institute of Education (Britton et al. 1975). Holland (1968) has commented on the fact that the detached nature of artistic experience, calling for no action on our part, is one of the most important factors in allowing us to be drawn more deeply into it.

7. Frye (1957) puts it more strongly: "The principle of manifold or 'polysemeous' meaning, as Dante calls it, is not a theory any more, still less an exploded superstition, but an established fact" (p. 72).

8. Holland (1968), approaching such problems from the perspective of the psychoanalytic tradition, reaches a similar conclusion: "Usually, one cannot tell from an isolated paragraph whether a work is fiction or nonfiction. Yet our response to the two genres differs sharply. Therefore, it must not be the paragraph alone that shapes our response. Rather ... it is the expectation we bring to the paragraph that determines the degree to which we will test it against our everyday experience. If we think the paragraph speaks truth, we will check it for truth. If we think it speaks fiction, we will not" (p. 68). Vygotsky (1971) has made similar comments in his discussion of the psychology of art.

9. Hotopf (1965) has emphasized a related point: "If our views are not surface features—as though a writer has only to put a transfer on our brains—, if they have roots down into us, in order to change them or get new ones perceived, a reader may need to be dazzled, bludgeoned, and enticed to see what is before his nose" (p. 247). Rhetoric is one of our means for accomplishing that bludgeoning and enticing.

10. Examining advertising with a structuralist approach, Leymore draws some fascinating analogies between advertising and myth: "Far from changing values, it very much follows and upholds existing ones. Over and beyond this advertising (like myth), acts as an anxiety-reducing mechanism.... It reiterates the essential problems of life—good and evil, life and death, happiness and misery, etc.—and simultaneously solves them. To the constant anxieties of life, advertising gives a simple answer" (p. x).

11. The point is hardly new but is often forgotten. Smith (1968) has used a similar principle in explaining changing fashions in poetic style: "When a poetic style becomes too familiar or rigidly predictable, the

reader's expectations are too completely controlled by, and satisfied in terms of, strictly literary conventions. In other words, when a poem becomes a closed system, it has nothing to say and nothing to reveal but the operation of its own laws. Its style has become a cliche and it is time for a poetic revolution, a renewal of the relation between poetic style and speech" (pp. 29–30). Zivin (1974) has demonstrated how verbalization can lead to satiation even in the play of five- to seven-year-olds, when they are asked to imagine all possible actions with a toy with which they are later allowed to play.

Chapter Three

1. Here we can cite good authority; cf. Koestler (1964): "Literature begins with the telling of a tale" (p. 301).
2. Thus Langer (1953): "The poet's business is to create the appearance of 'experiences', the semblance of events lived and felt, and to organize them so they constitute a purely and completely experienced reality or piece of *virtual life*" (p. 212). Langer argues that each of the arts creates its own special kind of "virtual" experience. Smith (1968) and Frye (1957), both approaching the problem from the perspective of literary criticism, have reached strikingly similar conclusions. In Smith's words, "we may conceive of a poem as the imitation or representation of an utterance" (p. 15).
3. Luria and Vinogradova (1959) have experimentally verified the extent to which sound predominates over semantic associations for young children, and have drawn parallels with the performance of mentally retarded and fatigued adults.
4. In the full transcriptions Weir gives the last word of this segment as "king" (p. 167); her discussions of the example earlier, however, suggest that "kink" is accurate.
5. Bateman (1967), studying humorous literature with six- to eleven-year-olds, found that the misuse of words leads the older child to a similar sense of superiority, with accompanying laughter.
6. Though this was true for this particular television series, another investigation indicated that television stories were not *in general* less real than other genres as far as these children were concerned. See Applebee (1973a, p. 370).
7. These forty-four children's knowledge of the origin of stories paralleled their belief in their truth. To the six-year-old, a story was something that came from a book. Many were aware that books come from shops and are made in factories, but finally, before the book there is another book. The proportion of children who eventually asserted that stories are "made up" by a real person rose from 30.8 percent at six to 95.5 percent at nine; chi-square=16.60, $df=1$, $p < 001$. Chi-square

for sex differences $=0.88$, $df=1$, ns. On tests of significance, see appendix 1.

8. During a preliminary study, wide discrepancies emerged in the extent to which children of the same age thought that stories were made up rather than "real"; in a few cases, this seemed related to disillusionment provided by more skeptical siblings. This was posed as a hypothesis for the main study, but was not supported by the data. None of the differences between six-year-olds with and without older siblings were significant, and most were not even in the predicted direction.

9. The NAEP (1973c) studies have examined the extent to which children at nine, thirteen, and seventeen, and young adults, share such a heritage by testing their ability to recognize specific works and characters on a variety of tasks. As one would expect, there is a general increase in performance with age, but there are also much greater regional and sex differences than usual on NAEP tasks. This seems to be a reflection of the development of regional and subcultural differences in the literary heritage. Boys, for example, excelled in identifying elements from adventure stories (for example, *Moby Dick, Treasure Island*) and heroes such as Daniel Boone and John Henry; girls did better with *Charlotte's Web, Winnie the Pooh,* and *Alice in Wonderland.* Such differences reflect the sex differences in reading preferences that have been found in the long series of interest studies (Mott 1970).

10. Chi-square for age $=12.69$, $df=3$, $p < .005$, two-tailed; chi-square for sex $=0.25$, $df=1$, ns. Conventional characters included both named characters (for example, Goldilocks) and unnamed characters of types peculiar, or nearly so, to the fantasy world (witches, cowboys). Statistics are based on the 120 story subsample described in appendix 1.

11. Following up earlier studies of adult expectations, Kuethe (1966) studied 600 children's books from his local library: 202 had a male with an animal, 91 had a female with an animal. Specific pairings were 67 boy-dog, 19 boy-cat, 25 girl-dog, and 26 girl-cat. There were no other gender-specific pairings. On the present results, see supplementary table 5, appendix 3.

12. This set of questions began with the declaration that, "When you hear a story about turtles, turtles in the story are usually very *slow,*" and went on to ask what each of the other characters was like. The six types were chosen on the basis of results from a preliminary study to provide a blend of real animals that children would have encountered in stories, as well as some characters whom they would have met only in fantasy. Responses to each character were ranked on four-point scales ranging from firmly defined expectations based on appropriate story roles, to descriptions based on real-life counterparts. For witches and fairies, the "real-life" end of the scale was defined as description of dress or appearance without assignment of role characteristics. Differences between the ages and sexes were tested by dichotomizing each score at its median. De-

tailed results are given in supplementary table 5, appendix 3.

13. The difference between animal and fantasy characters is significant at both six and nine, $p < .005$, using McNemar's test (Siegel 1956) to compare the number of children reflecting the adult expectation for at least one fantasy or animal character. Note that the analysis is concerned with specific expectations about the characters, whereas the earlier analysis was concerned with whether the children had any role expectation at all.

Chapter Four

1. These data are summarized in supplementary table 6, appendix 3. The multivariate F for age $= 42.1$, $df = 5;108$, $p < .005$.

   The T-unit (minimal terminable unit) is a measure formulated by Hunt (1965) as a more reliable index than the sentence, which fluctuates widely depending on the criteria used for punctuation. The T-unit is linguistically defined and, roughly put, involves segmenting the language into the shortest units which can stand on their own. T-unit length is directly related to linguistic complexity: the longer the T-unit, the more complex the language is likely to be in transformational terms.

2. Thus Smith (1968), discussing "Billy Boy," notes that it has many verses rarely heard in performance: "Although the opening and closing verses have thematic characteristics appropriate to their positions in the sequence, the central verses may be omitted or rearranged without affecting the thematic coherence of the whole song, and verses which provide additional variations on the common theme may be interpolated almost indefinitely: 'Can she drive a four-shift car? Does she have a Ph.D.?' and so forth" (p. 99).

3. Again Smith (1968) turned up many parallels in her analyses of adult poetry. See especially her discussion of what she calls sequential structure (pp. 109 ff.), where she notes that such chains can be based on logic or serial generation as well as time sequence.

4. The discriminant function analysis used fourteen variables: the five complexity measures, and the nine further characteristics summarized in supplementary table 7. Of the 120 stories, 68.3 percent were correctly classified on the basis of posterior probabilities for group membership. All possible pairs of groups were significantly different from one another. The overall F for discrimination among the six groups on the fourteen variables was also highly significant ($F = 4.56, df = 70;484.9, p < .001$).

5. Univariate effects were significant for number of words and number of characters, and nearly so for number of T-units. The data are reported in detail in supplementary table 7, appendix 3. In an analysis of variance without the covariance adjustment for age, all of these measures showed highly significant differences between plot structures.

6. There are also important developmental constraints on the ability to predict what comes next in an unfamiliar story; see chapter 7.

Chapter Five

1. Characters, action, and setting were independently rated for the degree of fantasy involved, defining fantasy as distance from the world of the child's immediate experience. Stories often show differing levels of fantasy in these three areas. Thus Cramer's V between fantasy in character and action $=.40$, between fantasy in character and setting $= .44$, and between fantasy in action and setting $= .65$. (On V as a measure of association, see Nie et al. 1975.)
2. There are of course many other, and important, means of distancing works of fiction. Those selected are simply an easy operationalization of selected aspects of form and involvement.
3. This judgment was made without reference to the *result* (for example, reward or punishment) of the actions. A second analysis assessed the apparent threat posed to the child by the material in the story. The resulting categorization, though not identical with that by acceptability of action, led to similar conclusions about the use of various techniques of distancing. It is reported in full in Applebee (1973*a*).
4. Frye (1957) has made a similar point, noting that the brutality of the crime story is "protected by the convention of the form, as it is conventionally impossible that the man-hunter can be mistaken in believing that one of his suspects is the murderer" (p. 47).
5. All of these data are summarized in full in supplementary table 9, appendix 3.

Chapter Six

1. Frye (1957) has made a very similar point, though he uses different terminology. See especially his discussions of value judgments (pp. 20 ff.) and of convention in art (pp. 99 ff.).
2. This formulation runs contrary to many previous studies of response. Purves and Rippere (1968), for example, treat evaluation as a separate response category parallel to their others, though the subcategories of evaluation parallel the major categories at least roughly. Cooper (1969), using their system, came to question this approach. One of his high school juniors commented that the other major categories "are the points you would use to explain why you liked or disliked the story" (p. 140).
3. Further details about samples and procedures are given in appendix 1. Six- and nine-year-olds were interviewed; nine- and thirteen-year-olds from a comprehensive high school and its drawing area received written measures; and thirteen- and seventeen-year-olds from a selective admis-

sions boys' school and girls' school received written measures.

During a preliminary study, a similar question included a list of possible points for discussion; this was abandoned after it became clear that many of the older children used the list as an outline of points to deal with in turn, often without any other structure to their response. The present procedure sought to discover what the students, rather than the investigator, thought was most relevant.

4. The children have no difficulty in making such nominations. The twenty-two six-year-olds cited eight different titles (mostly fairy tales); the twenty seventeen-year-olds cited eighteen (mostly novels). In a series of studies separately reported, children at these ages also nominated titles for a variety of other categories (Applebee 1976*b*). For specific titles cited frequently at each age, see supplementary table 2, appendix 3.

5. The distinction between summary and retelling here has an interesting parallel in descriptions of common characters, discussed in chapter 3. One set of responses from the forty-four children retold an incident in which the character participated: a lion "catches people" was the way Frederick C. (6 yr 1 mo) put it, and a fairy "gives people clothes." The other type of response categorized the character. Robert W. (9 yr 2 mo) was typical in his description of a fox as "terrible" and a fairy as "calm." In this sample, 72 percent of the six-year-olds and only 36 percent of the nine-year-olds used actions more than half the time to describe the roles of the six characters. Chi-square for age$=3.77$, $df=1$, $p<.05$, two-tailed; chi-square for sex$=0.11$, *ns.* On the calculation of statistics, see appendix 1.

6. Formal characteristics of the discussions are summarized in detail in supplementary table 10, appendix 3. For *Little Red Riding Hood,* scores on formal characteristics are based on discussions after prompting with a second question, "What happens in it?", and the numbers in each response category (retelling, summary, and so on) therefore do not correspond with results in table 3 (which are based on discussions without prompting).

7. Discussions analyzed in this and the following chapter were categorized using the five categories reported as well as transitional categories for stories showing a mix, for example, retelling/synopsis. These transitional categories were collapsed upward during data analysis as "any synopsis," "any summary," and so on.

8. In *Story poems,* selected and edited by Louis Untermeyer. New York: Pocket Library, 1957.

9. The difference was tested using a two-factor (age × sex) analysis of variance. F (age)$=25.14$, $p<.005$; F (sex)$=0.48$; F (interactions)$=0.06$; $df=1;40$ in each case.

10. The National Assessment system of analysis is based on that proposed by Purves and Rippere (1968), with an extension to include a separate category for retelling (which was part of perception in the original

system). Discussions of favorite stories in the present study were also scored during the Purves-Rippere system; results from that analysis are reported briefly in appendix 2.

11. Chi-square tests of differences between the two age groups for each of these measures were significant at the .05 level, two-tailed. On tests of significance, see appendix 1.

12. Comparing the two six-year-old samples, significantly more had difficulty responding to the wrong side of the bed than to the other saying. Chi-square $= 5.13$, $df = 1$, $p < .05$. On tests of significance, see appendix 1.

13. Chi-square for the difference between the sayings at age nine $= 11.88$, $df = 1$, $p < .001$. For the wrong side of the bed, there is a significant improvement in understanding between six and nine years (chi-square $= 23.22$, $df = 2$, $p < .005$). For the cat and mice, there is no significant difference in response at the two ages. On tests of significance, see appendix 1.

Chapter Seven

1. Machotka (1966), studying responses to color reproductions of paintings, found a similar concern with analysis. He pointed out the relationship to operational thought: "The criteria of style and composition appear to imply the hypothetical existence of several manners of representation, one of which ... seems the most satisfactory. The observer cannot judge style or composition if he knows only *one;* he can judge it only in comparison with others which, at the time of judgment, are imagined or hypothetical."

2. The difference between the written responses at age nine and the oral responses at the same age (table 3, chapter 6) may be an artifact of scoring procedures. The oral discussions were categorized directly from tape recordings, which provide an extra set of paralinguistic cues about what the child is trying to do; these are not available in the written answers.

3. The selective school pupils at age thirteen showed more evidence of analysis than did their comprehensive school peers. Ninety-five percent, compared with 50 percent of the comprehensive school pupils, gave some analysis of objective responses; 25 percent (versus 6.7 percent) analyzed their subjective responses; and 55 percent (versus 30 percent) analyzed the relationships between the two sets.

4. Analysis and generalization occur together in 23, analysis alone in 36, and generalization alone in only 4 of the 144 discussions (ages six to seventeen) of reasons for liking or not liking stories. Using McNemar's test of the significance of changes (Siegel 1956), chi-square $= 24.03$, $df = 1$, $p < .001$.

5. In the discussions in this and the previous chapter, reasons for liking

and disliking have been pooled. The question on liking produced more reasons than the question on disliking, while that on disliking led to an increase in the proportion of analytic, objective criteria as opposed to the other types.

6. Oral and written responses to the cat and mice at age nine are based on separate samples of children, and do not differ significantly from one another in either the proportion giving no response, or the proportion showing "any understanding," using Fisher's exact test (Siegel 1956).

7. Responses to the two sayings differed significantly at nine, and also significantly (but in the opposite direction) for all of the thirteen- and seventeen-year-olds pooled, using the McNemar test of the significance of changes (Siegel 1956). The birds of a feather saying is more obscure, raising vocabulary problems ("flock") and providing a less clear concrete situation to which analogies might be drawn.

8. This sort of response by analogy or exemplification is more likely to be encouraged in speech than in writing. This is usually justified as "making it relevant" or "seeing connections," but perhaps it should be given a more respectable function and encouraged more freely in writing as well as in speech at this age.

9. The nine countries were Belgium, Chile, England, Finland, Iran, Sweden, Italy, New Zealand, and the United States. The partition of Belgium into French-speaking and Flemish-speaking samples created ten populations. Sample sizes varied. Flemish speaking Belgium at the preuniversity grade had the smallest representation with 464 students; Italy at the preuniversity grade had the largest with 14,204 students.

10. There were also national differences, allowing the investigators to conclude that literary response is in substantial part learned. What seems to be most strongly influenced by patterns of schooling is the preferred school of literary criticism: "aesthetic" and "affective-interpretative" clusters of responses in England, for example, contrasted with "moral-symbolic" and "affective-moral" response clusters in the United States. On the effects of schooling on response patterns of adolescents, see Applebee (1977).

Chapter Eight

1. These arguments about the social nature of the process, and the underlying tension between the reader's and the writer's modes of construing, are, of course, equally true of transactional writing, though in that case the problem of direct versus vicarious experience does not arise in the same way.

Appendix One

1. Ames worked from the same research institute as Pitcher and Prelinger and drew from a nearly identical population in the years following their

study. Though more briefly reported, Ames' data provide useful amplification of the earlier work.

Appendix Two

1. Comparisons between studies are complicated by the fact that different baselines have been used for percentages reported. Data in the present study are based on computations of the proportion of responses in each category for each student; this produces average percentages for comparing groups. If percentages are based on the total number of statements produced by a group, results can be quite different. In the present study, for example, interpretation at seventeen rises from 19 to 33 percent simply by shifting to computations based on percentages of all statements.

Bibliography

Ames, Louise Bates. 1966. *Children's stories. Genet. Psychol. Monogr.* 73:337-96.

Applebee, Arthur N. 1973*a*. The spectator role: Theoretical and developmental studies of ideas about and responses to literature, with special reference to four age levels. Ph.D. dissertation, University of London. ERIC document ED 114 840. See *Resources in Education* 11 (1976).

———. 1973*b*. Where does Cinderella live? *Use of English* 25:136-41+.

———. 1974. *Tradition and reform in the teaching of English: A history.* Urbana, Ill.:National Council of Teachers of English.

———. 1975. Developmental changes in consensus in construing within a specified domain. *Brit. J. Psychol.* 66:473-80.

———. 1976*a*. The development of children's responses to repertory grids. *Brit. J. Social Clin. Psychol.* 15:101-2.

———. 1976*b*. Children's construal of stories and related genres as measured with repertory grid techniques. *Res. Teaching English* 10:226-38.

———. 1976*c*. Skill in the arts: The functions and development of presentational symbolism. ERIC document ED 131 496. See *Resources in Education* 12 (1977).

———. 1977. The elements of response to a literary work: What we have learned. *Res. Teaching English* 11:25–71.

Bannister, D., and Mair, J. M. M. 1968. *The evaluation of personal constructs.* New York: Academic Press.

Bateman, Robin. 1967. Children and humorous literature. *School Librarian and School Library Rev.* 15:153-61.

Berger, Peter L., and Luckmann, Thomas. 1966. *The social construction of reality: A treatise in the sociology of knowledge.* New York: Anchor Books. 1967 ed.

Beshai, James A. 1972. Content analysis of Egyptian stories. *J. Social Psychol.* 87:197-203.

Bettelheim, Bruno. 1976. *The uses of enchantment: The meaning and importance of fairy tales.* New York: Alfred A. Knopf.

Billow, Richard M. 1975. A cognitive developmental study of metaphor comprehension. *Develop. Psychol.* 11:415-23.

Blom, Gaston E.; Waite, Richard R.; and Zimet, Sara G. 1970. A motivational content analysis of children's primers. In *Basic studies on reading,* ed. Harry Levin and Joanna P. Williams, pp. 188-221. New York: Basic Books.

Bock, R. Darrell. 1963. Programming univariate and multivariate analysis of variance. *Technometrics* 5:95–117.

Bock, R. Darrell, and Haggard, E. A. 1968. The use of multivariate analysis of variance in behavioral research. In *Handbook of measurement and assessment in behavioral sciences,* ed. Dean K. Whitla. Reading, Mass.: Addison-Wesley.

Boyd, Nancy A., and Mandler, George. 1955. Children's responses to human and animal stories and pictures. *J. Consult. Psychol.* 19:367–71.

Britton, James N. 1954. Evidence of improvement in poetic judgment. *Brit. J. Psychol.* 45:196–208.

———. 1968. Response to literature. In *Response to literature: Papers relating to the Anglo-American Seminar on the Teaching of English,* ed. James R. Squire, pp. 3–10. Champaign, Ill.: National Council of Teachers of English.

———. 1969. Talking to learn. In Douglas Barnes, James Britton, Harold Rosen, and the London Association of Teachers of English. *Language, the learner, and the school,* pp. 79–115. Harmondsworth, England: Penguin Books.

———. 1970. *Language and learning.* London: Allen Lane The Penguin Press.

———. 1971a. What's the use? A schematic account of language functions. *Educational Rev.* 23:205–19.

———. 1971b. The role of fantasy. *English in Education* 5: 39–44.

———. 1973. Teaching writing. Paper prepared for the S.S.R.C. Research Seminar on Language and Learning, Scottish Council for Research in Education, Edinburgh, January 1973.

Britton, James N.; Burgess, Tony; Martin, Nancy; McLeod, Alex; and Rosen, Harold. 1975. *The development of writing abilities: 11 to 18.* London: Macmillan Educational, for the Schools Council.

Brown, Roger. 1958. *Words and things.* New York: The Free Press.

Bruner, Jerome S. 1968. *Processes of cognitive growth: Infancy* (1968 Heinz Werner Lecture). Worcester, Mass.: Clark University Press.

———. 1973. Organization of early skilled action. *Child Develop.* 44:1–11.

———. 1974. *Beyond the information given: Studies in the psychology of knowing.* London: George Allen and Unwin.

————. 1975. From communication to language: A psychological perspective. *Cognition* 3:255–87.

Bruner, Jerome S.; Goodnow, Jacqueline J.; and Austin, George A. 1956. *A study of thinking.* New York: John Wiley and Sons.

Bruner, Jerome S.; Olver, Rose; and Greenfield, Patricia M. 1966. *Studies in cognitive growth: A collaboration at the Center for Cognitive Studies.* New York: John Wiley and Sons.

Bullough, Edward. 1912. "Psychical distance" as a factor in art and an aesthetic principle. *Brit. J. Psychol.* 5:87–118.

Burke, Kenneth. 1945. *A grammar of motives.* New York: Prentice-Hall.

————. 1950. *A rhetoric of motives.* Berkeley and Los Angeles: University of California Press.

————. 1957. *The philosophy of literary form: Studies in symbolic action,* rev. ed. New York: Vintage Books.

————. 1966. *Language as symbolic action: Essays on life, literature, and method.* Berkeley and Los Angeles: University of California Press.

Cappa, Dan. 1958. Kindergarten children's spontaneous responses to storybooks read by teachers. *J. Educational Res.* 52:75.

Carlson, Patricia, and Anisfeld, Moshe. 1969. Some observations on the linguistic competence of a two-year-old child. *Child Develop.* 40:569–75.

Case, Duncan, and Collinson, J. M. 1962. The development of formal thinking in verbal comprehension. *Brit. J. Educational Psychol.* 32:103–11.

Cassirer, Ernst. 1944. *An essay on man: An introduction to a philosophy of human culture.* New Haven, Conn.: Yale University Press.

Cazden, Courtney B. 1972. *Child language and education.* New York: Holt, Rinehart, and Winston.

Cermak, Laird S.; Sagotsky, Gerald; and Moshier, Carroll. 1972. The development of the ability to encode within evaluative dimensions. *J. Exp. Child Psychol.* 13:210–19.

Chukovsky, Kornei. 1963. *From two to five.* Berkeley and Los Angeles: University of California Press.

Cooper, Charles R. 1969. Preferred modes of literary response. Ph.D. dissertation, University of California at Berkeley.

Cramer, Phebe, and Hogan, Katherine A. 1975. Sex differences in verbal and play fantasy. *Develop. Psychol.* 11:145-54.

D'Arcy, Pat. 1973. *Reading for meaning.* 2 vols. London: Hutchinson Educational, for the Schools Council.

DeBoer, John James. 1938. The emotional responses of children to radio drama. Ph.D. dissertation, University of Chicago.

Dixon, W. J. 1968. *BMD: Biomedical computer programs.* Berkeley and Los Angeles: University of California Press.

―――. 1970. *BMD: X-series supplement.* Berkeley and Los Angeles: University of California Press.

Dunsdon, M. I., and Fraser Roberts, J. A. 1955. A study of the performance of 2,000 children on four vocabulary tests. *Brit. J. Statistical Psychol.* 8:3-15; 10:1-16.

Dysinger, Wendell S., and Ruckmick, Christian A. 1933. *The emotional responses of children to the motion picture situation.* New York: Macmillan Co.

Flavell, John H. 1963. *The developmental psychology of Jean Piaget.* Princeton, N.J.: D. Van Nostrand.

Freidson, Eliot. 1953. Adult discount: An aspect of children's changing tastes. *Child Develop.* 24:39-49.

Frye, Northrop. 1957. *Anatomy of criticism: Four essays.* New York: Atheneum. 1967 ed.

Gardner, Howard, and Gardner, Judith. 1971. Children's literary skills. *J. Exp. Education* 39:42-46.

Gardner, Howard; Kircher, Mary; Winner, Ellen; and Perkins, David. 1975. Children's metaphoric productions and preferences. *J. Child Language* 2:125-41.

General Registry Office. 1966. *Classification of occupations.* London: Her Majesty's Stationery Office.

Goldman, R. J. 1965. The application of Piaget's schema of operational thinking to religious story data by means of the Guttman scalogram. *Brit. J. Educational Psychol.* 35:158-70.

Griffiths, Ruth. 1935. *A study of imagination in early childhood and its function in mental development.* London: Routledge and Kegan Paul.

Harding, D. W. 1937. The role of the onlooker. *Scrutiny* 6:247-58.

―――. 1962. Psychological processes in the reading of fiction. *Brit. J. Aesthetics* 2:133-47.

―――. 1968. Practice at liking: A study in experimental aesthetics. *Bull. Brit. Psychol. Soc.* 21:3-10.

Harms, Jeanne M. 1972. Children's responses to fantasy in relation to their stages of intellectual development. Ph.D. dissertation, Ohio State University.

Helson, Ravenna. 1973. Through the pages of children's books. *Psychol. Today* 7:107-17.

Holland, Norman. 1968. *The dynamics of literary response.* New York: Oxford University Press.

————. 1975. *Five readers reading.* New Haven, Conn.: Yale University Press.

Hotopf, W. H. N. 1965. *Language, thought, and comprehension: A case study of the writings of I. A. Richards.* London: Routledge and Kegan Paul.

Hourd, Marjorie L., and Cooper, Gertrude E. 1959. Coming into their own: A study of the idiom of young children revealed in their verse-writing. London: Heinemann.

Hunt, Kellogg W. 1965. *Grammatical structures written at three grade levels.* Research report 3. Champaign, Ill.: National Council of Teachers of English.

Inhelder, Bärbel, and Piaget, Jean. 1958. *The growth of logical thinking from childhood to adolescence.* London: Routledge and Kegan Paul.

International Labor Office. 1958. *International classification of occupations.* Geneva: International Labor Office.

Jakobson, Roman. 1960. Closing statement: Linguistics and poetics. In *Style in language,* ed. Thomas A. Sebeok, pp. 350-77. New York: M.I.T. Press.

Jones, Anthony, and Buttrey, June. 1970. *Children and stories.* Oxford: Basil Blackwell.

Karmiloff-Smith, Annette, and Inhelder, Bärbel. 1975. "If you want to get ahead, get a theory." *Cognition* 3:195-212.

Kelly, George A. 1955. *The psychology of personal constructs.* 2 vols. New York: W. W. Norton and Co.

Koestler, Arthur. 1964. *The act of creation.* New York: Macmillan Co.

Kuethe, James L. 1966. Perpetuation of specific schemata in literature for children. *Psychol. Rep.* 18:433-34.

Kuhn, Thomas S. 1962. *The structure of scientific revolutions: International encyclopedia of unified sciences,* vol. 2, no. 2. Chicago: University of Chicago Press. 1970 ed.

Langer, Ellen J., and Abelson, Robert P. 1972. The semantics of asking a favor. *J. Pers. Social Psychol.* 24:26-32.

Langer, Susanne K. 1942. *Philosophy in a new key.* Cambridge: Harvard University Press. 1969 ed.

———. 1953. *Feeling and form.* London: Routledge and Kegan Paul.

———. 1967, 1972. *Mind: An essay on human feeling,* vols. 1 and 2. Baltimore, Md.: Johns Hopkins University Press.

Levi-Strauss, Claude. 1966. *The savage mind.* London: Weidenfeld and Nicolson.

Leymore, Varda Langholz. 1975. *Hidden myth: Structure and symbolism in advertising.* New York: Basic Books.

Luria, A. R., and Vinogradova, O. S. 1959. An objective investigation of the dynamics of semantic systems. *Brit. J. Psychol.* 50:89–105.

Lyons, John. 1969. *Introduction to theoretical linguistics.* New York: Cambridge University Press.

McCreesh, J. 1970. The child's concept of the tragic. *Educational Rev.* 22:254–62.

McGhee, Paul E. 1971. The role of operational thinking in children's comprehension and appreciation of humor. *Child Develop.* 42:733–44.

Machotka, Pavel. 1966. Aesthetic criteria in childhood: Justifications of preference. *Child Develop.* 37:877–85.

Moffett, James. 1968. *Teaching the universe of discourse.* Boston: Houghton Mifflin.

Monson, Dianne L., and Peltola, Bette J. 1976. *Research in children's literature.* Newark, Del.: International Reading Association.

Morris, William Perot. 1970. Unstructured oral responses of experienced readers to a given poem. Ph.D. dissertation, Indiana University.

Mott, John Homer. 1970. Reading interests of adolescents: A critical study of fifty years of research. Ph.D. dissertation, University of Northern Colorado.

National Assessment of Educational Progress. 1973*a*. *Literature: Summary data.* Report 02-L-00. Washington, D.C.: U.S. Government Printing Office, for the Education Commission of the States.

———. 1973*b*. *Responding to literature.* Report 02-L-02. Washington, D.C.: U.S. Government Printing Office, for the Education Commission of the States.

———. 1973*c*. *Recognizing literary works and characters.* Report 02-L-03. Washington, D.C.: U.S. Government Printing

Office, for the Education Commission of the States.

Nie, Norman; Bent, Dale H.; and Hull, C. Hadlai. 1970. *SPSS: Statistical package for the social sciences.* New York: McGraw Hill Book Co.

Nie, Norman H.; Hull, C. Hadlai; Jenkins, Jean G.; Steinbrenner, Karin; and Bent, Dale H. 1975. *SPSS: Statistical package for the social sciences.* 2d ed. New York: McGraw Hill Book Co.

Peel, E. A. 1959. Experimental examination of some of Piaget's schemata concerning children's perception and thinking, and a discussion of their educational significance. *Brit. J. Educational Psychol.* 29:89–103.

———. 1964. The analysis of preferences. In *Research design and the teaching of English,* ed. David H. Russell; Margaret J. Early; and Edmund Farrell. Champaign, Ill.: National Council of Teachers of English.

———. 1966. A study of differences in the judgments of adolescent pupils. *Brit. J. Educational Psychol.* 36:77–86.

Piaget, Jean. 1926. *The language and thought of the child.* London: Routledge and Kegan Paul. 1959 ed.

———. 1929. *The child's conception of the world.* London: Routledge and Kegan Paul. 1967 ed.

———. 1951. *Play, dreams and imitation in childhood.* London: Routledge and Kegan Paul. 1962 ed.

Pitcher, Evelyn Goodenough, and Prelinger, Ernst. 1963. *Children tell stories: An analysis of fantasy.* New York: International Universities Press.

Polanyi, Michael. 1958. *Personal knowledge.* London: Routledge and Kegan Paul. 1962 ed.

———. 1969. *Knowing and being,* ed. Marjorie Grene. London: Routledge and Kegan Paul.

Purves, Alan C., and Beach, Richard. 1972. *Literature and the reader.* Urbana, Ill.: National Council of Teachers of English.

Purves, Alan C.; Foshay, Arthur W.; and Hansson, Gunnar. 1973. *Literature education in ten countries.* Stockholm: Almquist and Wiksell.

Purves, Alan C., and Rippere, Victoria. 1968. *Elements of writing about a literary work.* Research report 9. Champaign, Ill.: National Council of Teachers of English.

Raven, J. C. 1965. *Guide to using the Mill Hill Vocabulary Scale with the Progressive Matrices Scale.* London: H. K. Lewis.

Richards, I. A. 1924. *Principles of literary criticism.* London: Kegan Paul, Trench, Trubner and Co. 1945 ed.

―――. 1929. *Practical criticism: A study of literary judgment.* London: Kegan Paul, Trench, Trubner and Co. 1946 ed.

Sacks, Harvey. 1972. On the analyzability of stories by children. In *Directions in sociolinguistics,* ed. John J. Gumperz and Dell Hymes. New York: Holt, Rinehart, and Winston.

Sapir, Edward. 1966. *Culture, language, and personality.* Berkeley and Los Angeles: University of California Press.

Siegel, Sidney. 1956. *Nonparametric statistics for the behavioral sciences.* New York: McGraw Hill Book Co.

Smith, Barbara Herrnstein. 1968. *Poetic closure: A study of how poems end.* Chicago: University of Chicago Press.

Snedecor, George W., and Cochran, William G. 1967. *Statistical methods.* 6th ed. Ames: Iowa State University Press.

Squire, James R. 1964. *The responses of adolescents while reading four short stories.* Research report 2. Champaign, Ill.: National Council of Teachers of English.

―――. 1969. English literature. In *Encyclopedia of educational research,* ed. Robert L. Ebel, pp. 461–73. 4th ed. New York: Macmillan Co.

Sternglanz, Sarah H., and Serbin, Lisa A. 1974. Sex role stereotyping in children's television programs. *Develop. Psychol.* 10:710–15.

Vygotsky, L. S. 1962. *Thought and language.* Cambridge, Mass.: M.I.T. Press.

―――. 1971. *The psychology of art.* Cambridge, Mass.: M.I.T. Press.

Watts, A. F. 1944. *The language and mental development of children.* London: George G. Harrap and Co.

Weir, Ruth Hirsch. 1962. *Language in the crib.* Janua Linguarum Series Maior 14. The Hague: Mouton and Co. 1970 ed.

White, Dorothy. 1954. *Books before five.* New York: Oxford University Press, for the New Zealand Council for Educational Research.

Williams, E.D.; Winters, L.; and Woods, J.M. 1938. Tests of literary appreciation. *Brit. J. Educational Psychol.* 8:265–84.

Willy, Todd G. 1975. *Oral aspects in the primitive fiction of newly literate children.* ERIC document number ED 112 381. See *Resources in Education* 11 (1976).

Wilson, James R. 1966. *Responses of college freshmen to three novels.* Research report 7. Champaign, Ill.: National Council of Teachers of English.

Winer, Ben James. 1962. *Statistical principles in experimental design.* New York: McGraw Hill Book Co.

Wolfenstein, Martha. 1946. *The impact of a children's story on mothers and children.* Monographs of the Society for Research in Child Development, vol. 11, no. 1.

Zivin, Gail. 1974. How to make a boring thing more boring. *Child Develop.* 45:232–36.

Index

cence, 109–14; nature of, 90; reasons for positive, compared with negative, 141, 185–86 n

Evidence, lines of in studies of literary response, 90–91

Exemplification, 115–17, 125; encouragement of, in writing assignments, 186; incidents as, of whole story, 101; in story completion tasks, 122

Expectations: about fiction, 179 n; about spectator and participant roles, 17–18, 133; about story characters, 47–51, 181–82 n; about story form, 79; children's, reflected in their stories, 36, 138–41; derived from narrative form, 67–70; origin of, in previous experience, 3; study of cultural, 83. *See also* Representation of experience

Experience: broadening of child's, 74–76; decontextualization of, 130–31; effect of, on representations, 3; literary, 14, 77; literature and, 128–29, 132–33; nature of, in spectator and participant roles, 17–18; ordering of, in child language, 34–35; practical, as basis of concepts, 62; relationship of expressive to new, 23, 26; relevance of, to reader, 21; shaping of, 51–52; transactional techniques and approach to, 13; unfamiliar in stories, 74–76; vicarious, 129, 186 n; virtual, 180 n. *See also* Elaborative choice; Objective experience; Subjective experience

Expressive mode, 6–7, 23, 25–27; beginning of, 6; in children's narratives, 38; in diaries and memoirs, 71; in face-to-face encounter, 178 n; in presleep monologues, 35; limitations of, 10

Fable, discussion and retelling of, 90, 96–98, 141, 184 n

Fairies in stories, 49–53, 164

Fairy tales, 3–4, 22, 133

Family: as setting for children's stories, 75–76, 85; struggle for possession within, 34–35

Fantasy, 74–76, 132–33, 162, 166–69, 183 n. *See also* Distancing; Reality

Favorite stories. *See* Discussions of stories

Fiction: as technique for distancing, 119; children's recognition of, 38–47, 52–53, 132, 141; difference in response to, compared with nonfiction, 179 n

Flavell, John H., 93, 178 n

Focused chain as a narrative form, 58, 60, 64–65, 67, 69, 166–67

Formalization in transactional language use, 11–13

Formal operational thought, 108–11, 117–18, 123–25, 132–33; relationship of, to analysis, 185 n; sampling of children to represent, 142

Formulation of response, model of, 123–25

Foshay, Arthur W., 120

Foxes in stories, 49–53, 164

Fraser Roberts, J. A., 143

Freidson, Eliot, 47, 121

Frye, Northrup, 178–80 n; relationship of literary experience to literary criticism, 14; role of conventions in literary experience, 36–37, 183 n

Galvanic skin response, 123

Gardner, Howard, 104, 117–18, 121–22

Gardner, Judith, 121–22

Generalization, 108, 110, 124–25, 184 n; effect of, on evaluation, 112–14; evidence of, in IEA studies, 120; in interpreting sayings, 115–17; in story completion tasks, 122; levels of meaning and, 114

General Registry Office, 148

Giants in stories, 48, 53, 133; children's acceptance of reality of, 43–45

Progressive education, 129
Proportionality schema, 118
Proverbs. See Sayings
Pseudoconcepts and narrative form, 64-65
Psychical distance. See Distancing
Punishment of bad behavior, 81-82
Puppet as transitional form in recognizing fiction, 43-44, 46
Purves, Alan C.: and IEA studies, 120; and Victoria Rippere, 148, 152-55, 173-74, 183-85 n; and Richard Beach, 91, 119, 140, 152

Questionnaires, 138, 140-42, 144-46, 159
Question wording in studying literary response, 96-97

Rabbits in stories, 49-51, 164
Rapport during interviews, 140
Raven, J. C., 143
Reaching behavior of infants, 19-20
Reader: author's means of control over the, 14; elaborative choice of the, 25, 131-32; use of text by, for own purposes, 21
Reading ability of students, 143-47
Reading interest studies, 181 n
Reality: confirmation through nonsense, 40-41, 84; maintenance through conversation, 26-27; of stories, 38-39, 52-53, 181 n; social construction of, 4; virtual, 30; See also Fantasy
Reciprocity, 5-6
Reconstruing in the spectator role, 129
Referential meaning in expressive mode, 6-7 .
Reformulation, 20-21, 131-32; distancing and, 80; expressive mode and, 26-27; successful, occurs once, 25
Relationships as basis of poetic techniques, 13-15, 56, 71-72
Reliabilities, 140, 148, 162

Repertory grids, 138, 142, 145-46, 159
Representation of experience, 2-7, 17-25; ability to verbalize, 122-23; model of developmental stages of, for spectator role, 123-25; primacy of, in spectator role, 128; story recognized by child as a, 39; techniques for, 11-15. See also Concrete operational thought; Formal operational thought; Preoperational thought
Response to literature: appropriate types of written, 117; control of, in poetic, 14-15, 19; curtailment in adolescence, 122; developmental constraints on, 131-35; development over course of narrative, 123; forms of, 88; learned, 186 n; model of stages in, 123-25; most important, 155; multidimensionality of, 17, 72; natural versus limits of, 135; objective, 89, 101-5, 111-15, 118-19, 131, 186 n; Purves-Rippere elements of, 98, 120, 152-55, 173-75, 187 n; relevance of experience determines, 21; stock, 51; study of, 119, 138, 140-42; subjective, 111-14, 101, 105, 131; transactional language in study of, 16; versus production, 88
Retelling: in children's discussions of stories, 92-93, 96, 105, 111, 123-25, 171-72; in describing roles of characters, 184 n; in National Assessment samples, 98, 119-20, 184 n; levels of meaning and, 114-15; movement away from, 154; when asked to make up a story, 139
Reversibility in narrative form, 69
Rhetoric, 18-19, 179 n
Rhythm, 31, 101
Richards, I. A., 24-51
Rippere, Victoria, 148, 152-55, 173-74, 183-85 n
Ritual, 22-23
Roles of story characters. See Characters